To my family for supporting my dreams...
To my sister for being my biggest fan...
To the friends who believed in me...
To my husband for being my best friend...
To my son who made me want better...
To the people who built my testimony and pushed me to grow...
To the God who made me strong enough...
Thank you,
~Danika~

Chapter 1

As I walk down the street, I look around me. Above me was a grey sky filled with clouds making me feel miserable. Pulling my coat closer around me, I shivered as I quickened my pace.

On the left, there's two boys and two officers who are putting them both in handcuffs for the third time this month. Surely one of them will be charged this time. I shook my head and looked down. I think to myself, *Aren't they tired of fighting?* As I walked along, I prayed for those two boys I probably wouldn't see in the fall when school started. 3 strikes. I prayed long and hard.

To my right, I hear the sounds of police sirens blaring. The reason why would be in the news tomorrow morning, I'm sure. I see a wire fence with a sign saying "KEEP OUT! ATTACK DOG ON PREMISES". I see a homeless man begging for money as he crawls out of his towel made tent. *The homeless shelter must have run out of room.* I look forward and see a giant waste basket that is the community park. As I entered this repulsive place, I saw plates, coffee cups, and bags littering its ground. Needles and spoons laid near the children's playsets. My neck began to ache from all of the shaking.

    Disgusted, I pulled my jacket up around my neck again and stormed off, trying to remember why I came by in the first place. Then my phone vibrated in my pocket. I looked to see who was calling and smiled. I felt a bit warmer. I pushed the green answer button and held the phone up to my ear. "Hi, Jess," I said, cheering up.

    "Hey, Sammi. Where are you?" Jess asked in his worried voice that made my heart flutter.

    I smiled. "I'm on my way. I got a little side tracked. I just left the park. I'll be at your house soon," I said as his house came into view. I ran up on his steps. I paused as I quietly opened the door to his house. Jess was right beside the door talking to me on the phone. He had no idea I was behind him. I hung up the phone and watched him take it from his ear and redial my number. I turned my volume up and waited for it to ring. He sat there silently, then jumped as he heard my ringtone. He turned around and laughed as he saw me standing in his doorway.

I smiled and ran to give him a hug. "Hi Jess. Are you excited for summer?" I asked.

"Definitely and for senior year." He kissed my cheek as he picked me up and spun me around in his arms. When he put me down, I walked over to his wooden kitchen table, took my coat off, and put it on the back of a chair. I sat down in the chair, relieved to sit on the plush cushion. Jess sat in the chair next to me and put his hand on mine. "What's bothering you?" he asked looking into my eyes.

Why can you read me so well? "Nothing," I replied. He just looked at me with a small grin tugging at his lips.

"What?" I asked, shrugging.

"No really. What's wrong?" he tried again.

I took a deep breath. "Fine. I'm just tired. On the way here Jared and Logan got arrested for fighting, again! Not to mention the sirens stuck in my head and that poor park. I see homeless people living on the streets. I honestly couldn't even tell if he was faking it for the money, or if he really was homeless. And to top it off, why was I called the N word yesterday?" I asked, truly hurt. I felt a stray tear fall down my face. I closed my eyes as my mind sucked me into a memory.

I was on my way to pick some eggs up from the store. I had just turned my street corner when a group of teens from school threw me dirty looks, and walked up to me. They stopped me dead in my tracks. There were two boys and three girls, all in my grade.

I tried to walk around them, but they just mirrored me. "I've got to be somewhere, so please excuse me," I said quietly looking down.

The taller, skinny girl looked me over. She was the glamour girl in the group. She had purple, flashy high heels on and a lace top. She had shorts on that I'm surprised hadn't gotten her arrested. This girl gave me trouble all the time.

Crystal began, "Wow, I see the nigger has nothing to say. Surprising. Why don't you just go back to where you came from?" The entire group laughed except for the tiniest girl. She had not laughed until the glamorous girl gave her a glare. She sighed and gave a meaningless laugh.

"I came from here," I whispered. I turned on my heel and walked away, only for them to follow suit. God, please help me, I prayed softly.

"Wow, wait up, Nigger! What do you think it was like when your ancestors had to pick cotton? I bet it hurt. I wish it was still like that. I, personally, would make you my maid. You'd wear a slave outfit which is probably nicer than the rags you wear now," Crystal said, adding wicked laughter.

I was so tired of this garbage. "Leave me alone, please. I was born here. I was raised here. I've got just enough right to be here," I replied softly to her as I turned *away and began to walk. Sadness dragging my soul down.*

    I flashed back to reality to see Jess staring at me intently. I realized a few tears had fallen from my eyes. I felt Jess wipe them away. I sniffled.

    "Listen, Sammi. Try not to let anyone's words get to you. I know that's easier said than done. I love you and hate to see you upset over some stupid people's words," he whispered, putting his hand on my chin. "You are you and you're beautiful for it. I'm here when you're ready to talk about it. And I do agree with you. I believe the world has gotten out of hand. What do you plan to do about it?" he questioned, then placed a small kiss on my forehead.

    I smiled, but then looked down at the beautiful, deep blue table cloth. It's design was intricate and mesmerizing. "What could one person do?"

    He picked my chin up and kissed me softly. "You'd be surprised what you could do if you put your mind to it. But you won't be alone. I'd be there too."

I smiled. "You think we could do something?" I looked up at him and squeezed his hand. "Do you really think we could make any difference?"

I saw something flicker in his eyes. "Me and you? We could do anything. This world does need changing. So what do you wanna do about it?"

I smiled. "As long as you're there with me, I'd try. But how would we even start? We're just two kids." I pondered.

"Well, why not there?" he said pointing out the window. "You were worried about the park so we can get our friends and clean up the park together." He brushed a stray piece of hair behind my ear.

"Could we actually make a difference cleaning the park?" I was still doubtful. I loved Jess and wanted to believe him, but what power did we have?

"Yes we could. I think we could make a difference if we cleaned that park without being eaten alive by whatever lives in there." He put on a goofy face and gave me a reassuring grin.

I giggled at his comment. "So when will this park-cleaning day be?" I asked curiously.

Jess smiled. "Are you busy Friday?"

Chapter 2

"Are you guys ready to clean?" I asked the line of 7 friends that came to help clean the park. They all had garbage bags at the ready. I smiled.

I heard a range of comments such as-
"Yes ma'am!
Yeah!
I guess so.
Let's do this!
Sure." And even-
"Can I go to the bathroom first?"

"Um. . . sure. Over there." I pointed to a portable bathroom. "Let's go!" I said to the ones ready to start. They went off in all directions picking up trash as they went. I found Jess and began picking trash up beside him. "It's a really beautiful day," I said, eagerness spreading through me. "Such sunny weather is a delicacy." I giggled.

"For sure," Jess agreed, looking up at the sky, then picked up what I think was a bag of chicken bones. He quickly threw it into his garbage bag. I picked up some needles with my gloves, careful not to poke myself. I looked up too and saw a clear blue sky. Not a cloud in sight. Wiping sweat off my forehead, I turned on music for Jess and I to listen to. An upbeat song played and I began to hum along. Jess smiled.

    I looked around as people's garbage bags were already getting full. Then I realized a couple of people stopped during their walks. They were all wide eyed and looked at us as if they had never seen this park being cleaned. My eyes scanned the crowd until I found a very familiar face, but there weren't four others surrounding her. The girl shook her head and made the letter 'N' with her fingers.

    I nudged Jess and nodded to the girl slowly. Once he looked, Crystal put away her 'N', smiled, and waved in a flirty fashion. Jess grabbed my hand and brought it to his lips. Then, he turned away from the girl. As soon as Jess turned his back, the girl made the 'N' again. I looked back down and started picking up beer cans. I felt too self conscious to continue looking around. I turned the current song up louder, trying to keep out of my head.

"Is that Crystal?" Jess asked me, looking from the corner of his eyes at the girl.

"Yeah Crystal was the one from Monday. Her and her possy. That's why she's making the letter N with her fingers," I said softly, picking up a plastic cup with some type of brown liquid in it. I dumped it out and put it in the trash bag. I continued as I began to focus on the lyrics.

> *It's a miracle,*
> *that I've made it this far.*
> *But this ain't because of me.*
> *Ain't no wishing on a star.*
> *My Father's working,*
> *all the day and night.*
> *Even when I can't go on*
> *He continues to fight.*

I paused as I saw Crystal walking closer to me. But instead of stopping at me, she nudged me, and walked past me. She then stopped at Jess. Jess smiled and greeted her, then turned around away from me. He walked a couple feet away and began to whisper to Crystal.

I looked to my friend, Alejandro Martinez, who was listening to the whole conversation. He threw me a thumbs up and kept his focus on the two. When Jess finished the conversation, Crystal gasped and stormed off quickly. "Hey Jess," I started, "what'd you say to her?" I asked.

He just smiled. "Nothing." He gave an innocent grin. He put his hands behind his back and looked up to the sky, whistling.

"Huh." I laughed. "Well, I'll be back. I need to talk to Alejandro for a second." I smiled and walked to Alejandro. "Hey, did you uh, happen to hear what Jess said to Crystal?" I held my hands in front of me.

His face lit up as he smiled and nodded. "Jesse said his girlfriend's birthday is coming up. He asked if she had any ideas on what to get you. Crystal frowned and said no. So then Jesse just laughed and said he had an idea. He said how someone said some not so nice things to you, and that he wanted to talk to them, and ask her not to call the most beautiful girl ever, that name or say any of those other things.'" Alejandro cleared his throat. I shifted my weight to my left leg, listening to every word as Alejandro continued. "'Jesse asked a favor from her and said to go home and look up the exact definition of that word.' He said that if you were one, then the world is ending. Then Jesse just looked at the girl. She gasped and walked away like she was really mad. She threw her hands up, too." Alejandro couldn't help but laugh. He went serious soon after though and looked at me. His brown eyes bore into me. "But hey, you okay? We didn't know you were still having issues like this."

I nodded, "Yeah I'll be okay. Thanks, Alejandro. I really appreciate it." I gave him a small hug.

"Don't hold that stuff in, okay Sam? You don't deserve that mess," he assured me as he hugged me back.

"Thanks Al. I walked back over to Jess, who turned toward me when I came back.

"Alejandro told you, didn't he?" Jess asked. He had a small, half smile.

"Yeah, but that was really sweet of you, Jess." I smiled and gave him a tight hug. "Thanks!"

"Of course. Just to be clear, though, that's not your birthday present." He smiled as we both continued picking up garbage. How's that for a romantic date?

Chapter 3

In a few minutes, I looked up again and saw the same group of people watching us. I saw a guy walk to my friend Abby who was picking up, what looked like, small white keys to a piano. I saw her lips begin to move but couldn't make out the words.

I looked over at Jess. He moved beside me and pointed at the man making his way over to us. I looked at Abby who waved and smiled as she continued picking up the trash.

The young man put his arm around my shoulders and said, "You must be the beautiful Samantha." I felt Jess grab my hand. I watched him closely. The reporter introduced himself. "Hello. I am Ted Cramer from "The Shaeffer Gazette" reporting team. You are Samantha, right?" he asked.

"I am Samantha Addams, but people call me Sam. This is Jesse Jackson," I turned to Jess. "He's my boyfriend." Jess gave a convincing grin, stepping a bit closer to me.

Ted pulled his phone out of his pocket and began voice recording. "Fantastic. I'd love to interview the two of you. Can you tell me why you are doing this?" he asked with a television smile. "Oh darn, one moment." He fidgeted with his phone for a moment.

"Okay," Jess said, mirroring his smile. I stuck my tongue out at him and smiled. He rubbed my hand in his. "You know, I think that's like the third time in our lives you have called me Jesse. It sounds kinda weird." He smiled again.

"It felt weird saying it," I giggled. I tried to calm my breathing as a lump rose in my throat. I tried to resist the urge to start shaking with anxiety from speaking with this reporter.

"So Sammi, Jesse, we have all known how over time this park has been abandoned. But you two teens seem ready to put an end to that nonsense." To us he asked, "How old are each of you?" He pointed the microphone our way.

"I'm seventeen and Sam's seventeenth birthday is in a few weeks," Jess answered calmly. He was made for a job on television. From his collected calmness to his beautiful smile.

"And just what are you and your friends planning on doing here today?" he asked, pointing the phone back to us.

I felt Jess squeeze my hand. It's time to tell all of Shaeffer how I felt. I took a deep breath to calm my insides. "We wanted to show what became of this poor park: a wastebasket." I forced myself to speak up. "The animals and plants didn't make this mess. We did. In the bible, Romans 1:20 says "God is clearly seen in His creation", but look what we have done to it. God gave us this earth. Why do we treat it with such disrespect? How can we expect to thrive as a community when the one place we have to walk away from the city and the noise is treated like this?" I took another breath waiting for Ted's response.

Ted looked at me, winked, and smiled. He looked back to his phone and said, "I have a feeling we'll be seeing a lot more of you. Nice meeting you two. I expect great things." He smiled and turned his voice recorder off. "I'm gonna get some shots of you and the kids working." Jess and I called everyone over for a group picture. The ten of us wrapped our arms around each other and smiled as Tedd snapped a picture. Then everyone went back to cleaning as he followed with his phone camera.

    I turned to Jess. He looked at me with a grin. "You did great, Sammi! You told everyone what you thought. I'm so proud of you! I know that was hard for you." He pecked my cheek.

    "Thanks," I said as I felt my cheeks heat up. "I just thought of what you said and spoke what God gave me to say. But I am a bit shaky still."

    "Well because you forced yourself out of your comfort zone, now everyone knows what you're doing." He winked at me.

    I gestured to us then to all of our friends. "Correction. What *we* are doing."

    We continued to pick up trash. After a few minutes, a small finger poked my back as I picked up what I think was a pizza box. I turned to look and saw the small girl that hung with Crystal.

    "Excuse me, I don't know if you'd remember me but I'm Mary Jones? I just have to say sorry the way Crystal treated you. She thinks it's funny when others feel bad about themselves," she paused as Jess came to stand behind me. She pushed her glasses up on the crook of her nose and continued, "I didn't want to laugh at you. But I would have been next. I hope you can find it in your heart to forgive me." She put her head down and her posture fell.

    I just watched for a second. She was a small girl, probably around 5 foot even. She had short blonde, gorgeous hair with streaks of brown through it. She had glasses and still dressed cute but not as flashy as Crystal. I smiled and said, "Don't worry about it. It didn't bother me that much." I waved my hand. I felt Jess rub my back gently.

    "Either way the way she treated you was cruel and very rude." Mary added, "I also wanted to tell you that most of us aren't like Crystal. We only hung out with her because... because.." she looked down. "I guess I don't even know why we hung out with her. But after the way she treated you, I told her what I thought. Then I left. Now

I'm here to apologize and see if maybe we could be friends and I could join?"

I nodded. "Of course. Grab a bag and get started wherever you'd like." I pointed at the pile of garbage bags and gloves on the bench next to the entrance of the park. They sat in a pile peacefully.

"Thank you," she smiled and hugged me. I returned the smile and thanked her for the apology. I assured her all had been forgiven and she walked towards the bags.

"Hey Sammi," Jess said, taking my hand and turning me towards him. "Everything okay?" he asked, pecking my forehead.

"Yeah," I smiled and leaned into him for a hug. "It looks like it will be."

Chapter 4

"Wow! So much trash. How are we going to get it all to the dump?" my friend, Ian Harold asked.

I had an idea. "Does anyone know someone with a truck who'd be willing to help." I asked, raising an eyebrow. A few people in the group raised their hands. "Well if you can, call them and see if they can help us get this to the community dumpsters on Third Street."

I watched as people took out their smartphones. I dialed my mom's number. My phone rang a few times then my mom answered. "Hey sweetie. What's up?" she asked

"Hi, Mom. I was wondering if you would be able to bring Daddy's old truck to the park to take some garbage to Third?"

"Of course, hun. I'll be there in a sec, bye." I sat stunned momentarily as mom was always so calm when I talked about my dad with her.

I hung up my phone. Mostly everyone else was off the phone as I slid mine back in my pocket. All eyes were on me. We ended up getting 4 trucks to come help load. I looked around. The park has never been so clean. You could see the benches and water fountains and walk without stepping in or on something. I smiled and closed my eyes to thank God for today. I smiled even more as I felt lips brush against my forehead. I opened my eyes to see Jess grinning at me. "We did it," he said, picking me up in a hug.

 I giggled as my feet left the ground. "We did, huh?" By this time, trucks began showing up. Teens took off grabbing bags of garbage. A boy ran up to Mary and gave her a small hug. He was also from Crystal's group. Dominic Myers said, "I thought my dad's truck could help you out. I wanted to say sorry about the way Crystal treated you. There was nothing I could say that would make it okay for me to allow it, but after Mary stood up to her, I was next. But anyway. My dad said we can help take this stuff over." He smiled and pointed to a red truck.

 "That's great." I responded. "And no worries, it's all in the past," I said, trying to keep away from the flashback. I looked to where the pile of trash bags was getting smaller and smaller. That's when I realized just how much trash was there. Everyone hauled our bags onto all the trucks. I found my dad's old green truck and took some garbage bags over to it with Jess. I stacked them in the back and watched her drive off. When we were finished, we met in the place the garbage bags had been.

"Thank you all so much for helping. The park looks like we can actually use it again," I said, smiling.

We all parted. Jess pulled his phone out and texted Mrs. Jackson he'd be home later. He grabbed my hand as we walked to my dad's truck my mom arrived back with. Jess opened the door for me, and he helped me up into it. I moved over to the middle next to my mom as he climbed in behind me. He put his arm around my shoulders. My mom just smiled at us.

"What's that for?" I asked, smiling back.

She started the truck up and pulled away from the curb. "Just proud of you both. And really good job on your speech, Sam. I read it in an article online for The

Shaeffer Gazette. When did you practice that?" she asked as she turned the wheel to the right, following her turn signal.

"I didn't." I shrugged my shoulders. I watched as my mom's mouth dropped. So I explained some more. "I thought about what Jess told me and said what God put in my mouth to say." I looked down, feeling shy as I always do when I talk about myself.

"She's always been gifted with words, Ms. Addams." Jess squeezed my shoulders and kissed my cheek. I placed my head on his shoulder and saw my mom watching us in the mirror, smiling to herself. I put my hand on her knee and she rubbed it with one of her hands.

As we pulled into our driveway, I finally felt my shoulders relax as they untensed. I felt safe.

Chapter 5

My mom looked at the clock we had on the wall. It was five o'clock. She shook her head and continued. "Well, I've got to get back to work. I was only able to have a break for a little while. I should be back around ten tonight. Mrs. Isabella said you could eat with them tonight. Behave you two." She stood up, stretched, kissed me and Jess' foreheads, and walked to the front door.

I watched the door close and looked at Jess. "So, how do you think we did?" I curiously asked, sitting up straighter to face him.

"I think we did what we wanted to and more." He kissed my cheek.

"You wanna be my brownie taste tester?" I asked, sitting up.

"If you're making them, they might not last long." He laughed.

I stood up and led him to the kitchen and pointed at the stool for him to sit at the counter across from me. I grabbed the flour, sugar, butter, eggs, milk, and oil and set them in front of Jess. "Jess, I wish we could have made a bigger difference," I said, cracking open three eggs. "Like a bigger difference than just Shaeffer Park. I want to change more than that." I stirred the eggs, sugar, and milk together.

"I know you do. So what's next on your list of changes?" he asked, drumming his fingers on the countertop.

"I don't know. There's so much to change I don't know where to start." I looked down at the bowl of brownie mix. "Next in a little while, I want us to raise money for the homeless shelter to build on to it's complex. I saw a homeless man Tuesday. I figured the shelter ran out of room." I pulled out a cake pan and poured the batter into it leaving a small amount in the bowl.

"That's a great idea," he stated as I handed him the remainder of the bowl. I stuck my index finger in it and tapped his nose. Jess laughed.

"Are they good?" I giggled and wiped the batter off his nose and smeared it on his lips.

Jess grabbed hold of my waist and placed his brownie-mix lips against mine. He pulled away and licked his lips to taste. "Yum," he mumbled, grabbing the bowl for the remainder.

"Thanks. You know, you were getting a bit jealous a few times today?" I gave an over exaggerated concerned look. Then smiled.

"I wasn't. I was just ...um... concerned," he tried to pass off. He looked everywhere but at my eyes.

Words dripping with sarcasm and dragging each word, I said, "Okay sure, Mr. Linebacker."

....

"Hello, Sammi!" I snapped out of my head and realized I was staring at the floor. My heart was beating painfully and my head was spinning. I put my head in my hands for a moment and rubbed my eyes. I sat up and looked at Jess who sat beside me, his hands resting on either side of his legs. He sat sitting straight up and tense, trying to keep a calm face. "Do you need a minute?" he asked. He coughed a bit and looked down. I looked back down and nodded. *Ground yourself. You're with Jess.*

You're safe. I stayed silent trying to breathe. I followed the lines of the floorboards, spinning my ring on my pointer finger. "Let me know when it's okay to hug you," Jess said quietly. "And when you're ready to talk." I nodded again.

He got up from the couch and walked to the kitchen. I heard the sink turn on and off and the freezer opened. He returned with a cold glass of ice water and sat it on the table to the left of me. Silently, he left out his screen door that led to the back yard. I let a few tears fall as guilt and embarrassment began to well up. My throat felt as though it was going to close. *It's your fault, Sam. You deserved it. Jess will never really love someone who's used.* I cried as the thoughts swirled around my head. I put my head in my hands. *What is wrong with me? I should be over all this already. Grow up, Sam. Get over it. You're being a baby.*

Eventually my mind stopped spinning and my tears ran out. My eyes were dry and my chest felt tight. I got off the couch and walked into the kitchen to the bathroom. I closed the door behind me and leaned over the sink and looked at myself in the mirror. My mind began pointing out every flaw I saw in myself. My fat nose, big eyes, small ears, curly hair, broad man-like shoulders, my big lips, my ugly brown eyes, my light caramel skin. I looked away from the mirror, hating what I saw, and looked down to my hands holding the sink. My man hands, my long scrawny arms, the scars. I brushed my fingers along my left arm. I shook my head and turned the sink on to splash some cold water on myself.

    I turned off the sink and dried my face on the hand towel. I took a few deep breaths to slow my breathing and braced myself to face Jess. I walked through the house and to the screen door. I saw Jess throwing some fish food into the coy pond. He stopped for a moment and put his hands on his head. His back muscles pulled tight as he let out a deep breath and looked up to the sky. Pushing my guilt down, I opened the door and walked out to his backyard, sitting in the grass a few feet from the pond. Jess turned and came to sit beside me, leaving some space between us. He wrapped his arms around his legs, his feet slightly stretched in front of him.

We sat in silence for a few minutes listening to the pond waterfall cycle water and feeling the breeze hit our faces. "Hey, Jess?" I finally got the courage to ask.

"Yeah?" he replied.

Picking at the grass in front of my crossed legs, I whispered, "How can you want to be with me?"

"What do you mean?" he questioned me.

I took a breath, tying two pieces of grass together. "How can you want to be with me? I'm such a mess." I felt tears prick my eyes yet again and blinked a few times to get rid of them.

"Because I love you, Sammi. You're my best friend and have always been here for me. You're my perfect match. Where I struggle, you keep me strong. You help me want to be better. You help me stay on the right path. And you love God? I'm actually lucky you want to be with me." I saw him from the corner of my eye cross his legs and start brushing grass off his shoes. "Why wouldn't I want you?"

My eyes got hot again. "Because I'm all... used," I whispered. I felt tears threaten to fall, so I turned my head away from Jess to look at the road through his chain-link fence. I watched as cars drove past, people walking along to the park, kids going by on bikes and scooters.

"Sammi," Jess began softly. "Were you there?" He cleared his throat and continued, "During your flashback? Were you... with him?" I finally brought myself to face Jess. His eyes were soft, his face concerned. I nodded. Jess went silent and we both turned back to the pond.

"How can you want someone after something like that? I'm not pure anymore. I'm used and dirty." I asked, feeling a deep cut in my heart. I wanted to throw up, but held the urge in.

Jess shook his head. "He's a piece of shit, Sammi." After a moment, he whispered "Sorry. A piece of trash." I saw him clench and unclench his fists as he stared straight ahead. "It wasn't your fault, Sammi. And you aren't used. You aren't a damaged girl, unworthy of love. Isaac deserves to rot for what he did to you." I looked at Jess as he ran his hand through his hair and then rubbed the back of his neck. I swallowed the knot in my throat and slid over next to him leaning my head on his shoulder. "Is it okay?" he asked. I nodded. He let out a sigh of relief and wrapped his arms around me gently. He kissed my head for a long time. "I'm sorry, Sammi," he whispered against my head. "I love you so much. I'm so sorry."

Chapter 6

"Hey, you. Stop!" came a young boy's voice from behind Jess and I. I looked around the park, then to Jess. We slowly turned to see a kid around our age coming to meet us. He had blonde hair that flipped off to the left side, blue eyes, a red band tee, blue jeans, and blue sneakers.

"Hi," Jess said politely, putting his hand out for the teen to shake.

The teen just glared at it and asked, "Are you religious? I saw your interview in the paper. The scriptures," he inquired. He raised an eyebrow at us.

Jess and I automatically nodded our heads. "We are Christians," I stated clearly. "We don't consider ourselves "religious" though. Religion is following a bunch of man made rules and rituals. We just love God and want to do His Will."

"Same difference. You people are awful." He crossed his arms and glared at us.

"Well how come?" I asked in a kind voice. I put my hand on his shoulder. The boy shrugged it off and turned his back to us. "Because all you Christians hate people like me."

I was shocked. "Why would we hate you? Or anyone like you?" I asked walking around to face him.

He again turned, but realizing he faced Jess, turned back around towards me. "I'm gay. Christians hate us because we are who we are." He scoffed.

I felt heat rush to the back of my eyes. "Who told you that?" I put my hands on both of his shoulders so he couldn't turn away. He just looked at me. "Who?" I asked, lowering my voice slightly.

"TV, churches, our parades, everywhere you see people hating us. Mostly the religious people." He looked down to his blue sneakers.

"That's not true. We don't hate you or anyone like you. We are to hate sin. Not the person behind it. We do not hate gay people. Whoever told you that is lying to you." I said pointing to Jess. "I promise you we do not hate you. We would never hate you because you like the same sex. I'd be the one sinning if I chose that." I gave a small smile hoping I got through to the boy.

"I believed in God, but people tell me I can't if I am what I am." He got quieter.

"That's not true either. I know I am a christian who sins. I'm not perfect and what's amazing is I don't have to be perfect. God just wants my heart, not perfection." I took my hands from his shoulders. I felt Jess's hand on my hip as I watched the boy.

He looked confused and like he was thinking hard. His eyes would flick up at me, then back to the ground, over to a nearby tree, and back to me. "But God doesn't love me," he whispered.

I felt my heart shatter. How could he feel that way? Jess squeezed my hip and I looked at him. He looked affected too. He mouthed, 'Let me take this one'. I did as I cuddled up to him, sadness taking over this beautiful summer Saturday.

"What's your name?" Jess asked calmly.

"Alex," the boy said.

"Alex, whoever told you such a thing was lying to you. Do you really believe God cares
nothing about you?" The arm that wasn't around me, Jess put that hand on Alex's shoulder.

Alex shrugged and looked down, turning the tip of his shoe in the dirt. "I don't know."

"Let me help you," Jess paused as a beautiful colored bird flew past us. "Romans 5:8 says 'but God shows his love for us in that while we were still sinners, Christ died for us.' Take away the 'being gay'. People love to pick and choose which sins are worse than others. I can't even keep my own sin in check. Anger, guilt, unforgiveness... Those are my sins I have to work on because they keep me from loving my neighbor as Jesus calls me to," Jess paused and rubbed his neck. "Everyone sins and none are above others. We are people who are called to love our neighbors. How can I help lead you to Christ when all I do is spew hate at you?"

Alex stood listening to Jess's every word. "But it says it's a sin."

Jess took a breath and looked to the sky, tightening his grip on me. "It does say it's a sin. But so is a hateful heart, so is putting anything above God, so is jealousy. And I personally believe there are spirits that we can be born with some sins already latched on to us from generational curses. I can't try to explain God. I would fail miserably and possibly end up hurting your walk by trying. I could do my best, but I'm only human. But I do know He loves you and wants nothing but the best for you. He has a plan for your life that you won't believe. It won't be easy, and some days, it'll seem much easier to not follow Him. But that's your decision to make. But know that no matter what you decide, we" he motioned between him and I, "will never hate you. And I'm sorry on behalf of all the hypocrites you've met to make you believe God hates you. Even if you decide you don't want to follow Him or give into this whole 'Christian' thing."

Alex moved his point of focus drastically, seeming confused and uncomfortable. "Doesn't he? I mean I've been taught there's something wrong with me. Maybe I'm gay for a reason but I'm not sure. I'm just confused. How could God want me?" he asked.

Jess let out a small breath. "Ya know? Broken, hurt, and confused people are exactly who He uses. What good would it be if He tried to use someone for change who had it all figured out? Who had the money and the means? How would that move the broken to Him? The little ones, the poor, the sick, the 'nobodys'." He took his arm from around me and added finger quotation marks. "Broken people are the best. They've lost the most, they've hurt the most, and they feel the most. That's who God wants to use the most. God wants a little boy named David. Not a giant, experienced fighter. The giant winning? That shocks no one. It turns no heads. But the little boy winning? Now that changes the game."

Chapter 7

"Over here Alex!" I called from the steps of Freedom Church. I waved him over.

"Hey. Are you ready?" Jess asked.

"I want to know what this love is. How this Guy can love me when I don't even know Him. When I don't even love myself." He took a deep breath and smiled. I looked at him and smiled back. He had khakis, a plaid button-up, with a tie and his same blue sneakers.

I looked at Jess who had a solid light blue button-up on, a necktie, khakis, and black shoes. I looked at my phone. We had ten minutes before church started. "Do you guys want to find a seat before church starts?" I asked snapping the boys out of their conversation.

"Can I sit somewhere not in the middle of the room, please?" Alex asked.

"Sure," Jess answered. He opened the door and held it open for Alex and then me as he followed behind.

We sat Alex in the first row far off to the left, right in front of where Jess and I stand. "Alex, we'll be up there if you need us. Okay?" I asked as he sat down.

He took a deep shaky breath, "Okay." I smiled at him and he smiled back. Jess and I went to the door next to the worship section and walked through it, meeting up with the rest of the members who were getting ready to pray. Including two new faces. Jess and I walked up to Mary and Dom. "You guys joined the team?? That's great!" I congratulated.

"We're joining, yes! We're starting practices this week. We just thought it was time to focus on fixing ourselves. I don't want to be known as a mean girl, even by association." Mary looked down with a guilty look. "We just wanted to find a new direction, ya know?"

I put my hand on her shoulder and smiled. "Well this is a great place to start," I paused as our worship leader, April, came in and announced it was time. She clapped her hands three times.

We all filed into line and I went to stand in front of Jess. As the music began to play we began walking out the door and into the main room. The crowd in the seats clapped and cheered as we swayed and made our way to the stage to join the band.

Miracles by Danni Jay was one of my favorite songs. We all began to dance and clap to the beat of the music. Before we started singing, I looked at Alex. He looked like it took all he had to not run.

"I did not know my purpose.
I did not know Your plan.
I denied Your goodness.
I quit and I ran."
. . . .

By the end of the song, I looked over to see Alex out of his seat clapping. He was still sheepish, but seemed to really be enjoying himself. My heart was full for Alex. I felt goosebumps as I felt my heart swell in a comfort I knew all too well. The Holy Spirit.

"Good morning and welcome to Freedom Church. This," Pastor Lee, the assistant pastor, paused and waved a hand at us, "is the youth performing with songs of praise. And let me say what a fine job they are doing today. Here's another selection I am very eager to hear. Bring your song on, youth!" Pastor Lee smiled and sat back in his seat to the right of us.

We all looked at the Worship leader as she smiled and began to clap, cuing us to follow. The music began to play. I looked over at Alex who was already out of his seat just like everyone else was. I smiled. I loved this song. The Answer by Nauddy Monet.

"Oooooh You're the answer.
Yeah You're the answer.

Those days you're walking round waiting for a purpose,
waiting for a call.
Wondering when you're gonna feel something.

Sitting and waiting for hope, for love.
Waiting for anything.

But now I've found the answer, answer, answer.

God You were my answer.
I've never felt a love like this before.
That chooses me over and over.
Now I've found the answer, answer.

There's nothing I can do to escape your love.
Nowhere I can run to hide from you above.
Nothing I can say to make You run away from me.

Waiting for a love like this forever, like this forever
that would love me as I am.

But now I've found the answer, answer, answer.
God You were my answer.
I've never felt a love like this before.
That chooses me over and over.
Now I've found the answer, answer

My past is left behind me.

My God will never hold it against me.

My future stretches forward, higher.

My Answer, He fights for me!

Now I've got the answer, answer, answer.

God You were my answer.

I've never felt a love like this before.

That chooses me over and over.

Now I've got the answer, answer.

Yeah I've got the answer."

As the song ended, I looked out at the crowd standing whistling and clapping. I tried to look at Alex. I spotted his blue sneakers and looked up seeing a smiling young man. It was still Alex, but there was just a difference.

"Amen, Amen, Amen! Let's give it up again for our youth. They are really something special. These young men and women are trying their hardest to set others free with the love of Jesus Christ. If any of you youth in the crowd would like to participate, please talk to April at the end of service. We would love to expand our team to help you join the ministry God calls you to." The assistant pastor nodded and smiled. "Now before we hear some more of their selections, let's get some announcements going. Andrea?" he motioned.

    She made her way up to the podium. "Good morning, church. First I'd like to welcome all the new members. I'd also ask, if you are a new member that doesn't have a church home, who would like this to be their home, please stand." She paused and waited for families to stand. "Welcome you new and bright men and women. And you young men and women. Thank you and you can see me or any other awesome person up here after service about plugging in to the ministry you'd like to join. In further news, The 'Freedom Women' retreat is on June 15. We will be holding it here this year, downstairs. The 'Faith Like Joseph' Men's retreat is the twenty-second, also here. Tom has all the details and a sign up sheet is in the back. For the fourth of July, the church will have a huge party in our yard to watch the fireworks. We'll have food, drinks, games, bounce houses, and prizes. So if you aren't busy, join us in a wonderful night full of fellowship. Amen?"

"Amen," a mumble rose from the crowd.

"Amen indeed. The Youth Group meets every Friday evening from 6-8pm. See Youth Pastor Angie for information. Those are all of my announcements and I wish you all a wonderful day. "Now it's my amazing job to give you another chance for ministry! Giving. Now though it is time to give your offerings, I'm not talking about just money. If you're not involved in something here, I encourage you to plug in somewhere to help reach lives. God loves you and has called you for this time and a purpose that is uniquely yours! So please bring forward your offering and gift to our awesome God and let's welcome Pastor Mae Thula!" The crowd cheered and some people came to drop envelopes off in the baskets on the left and right side of the front aisles.

The worship team and I applauded loudly. As we settled down, lead Pastor

Mae Thula walked on stage. "Now today, I'd like to talk about," she paused and grinned, "the unfailing and unwavering love of God. I have to tell you something about this lesson." She leaned forward. "God gave me this message yesterday after I finished the one I originally planned. He told me that someone today needed to hear it."

Chapter 8

"Oh Alex! I am so happy for you! I am so glad you gave your life back to the Lord. And to do it today. Congratulations!" I cheered as we walked out of the church. Jess by my right and Alex on my left.

Jess was also smiling. "Would you like to start meeting with someone from the church?" Jess paused for an answer.

"I would like just you guys for now, if that's okay. I have personal things I need to talk about with real friends," Alex replied. I saw new hope in his eyes. Passion flickered through him.

"Yeah, of course," I said. We got to the corner where Jess and I would split from Alex. "How's Tuesday for our first time?" I asked.

"Whatever day or time you guys can meet with me would be wonderful. Thank you guys so much! This means the world to me. I'll see you Tuesday," he said, as we parted ways.

"Tuesday at seven-thirty in the park. Bye!" I called.

"Bye!" he hollered.

Jess and I turned the corner and started off to his house. "Wow. That was amazing." I stopped as he tightened his grip on our intertwined hands.

He smiled. "Are you ready to help lead someone to Christ?" he asked.

I pondered. "If you are, I am. I am ready. What about you, Mr. Deep Questions?" I giggled a bit.

"Yes ma'am. I'm ready." He kissed my cheek and we crossed the street onto his block, continuing to walk on the outside of the sidewalk. We walked onto Jess's front porch and he turned me towards him taking both of my hands. "You sang amazing today. Words can't describe it." He smiled at me and raised an eyebrow. Our eyes and hands locked.

"Well, so did you. Your voice sounded wonderful today." I kissed his cheek.

"We are just a perfect harmony." I giggled as he made a goofy face, opened the door, and led me inside. We heard movement in the kitchen. "Hey, Aunt Isabella. Are you home?" We heard other voices as we walked into the kitchen.

"Yeah, hun. Uncle Frank will be home in a couple minutes. I just got in." Mrs. Isabella replied, giving Jess a kiss on the cheek as he towered over her by quite a few inches.

She gave me a tight hug. "Hi Sammi. Why don't you guys sit down and watch some TV while I finish lunch?"

"Yes, ma'am," I responded. She stepped out of the way of the small television set in the kitchen and turned the one on in the living room. I took my shoes off by the door, and followed Jess into the livingroom to the love seat. He put his arm around my shoulders, and I wrapped mine around his middle.

We heard the front door open and shut. Mr. Frank Jackson walked in, put his keys and bag on the table, and came to stand behind Mrs. Isabella. He wrapped her in a tight hug before coming in to sit with us. "So Jesse, do you have a CD for us?" Mr. Frank asked, walking into the dining room.

"Yes sir. It's on the counter next to the microwave." Jess turned to look back into the kitchen.

"Thanks, Jesse," Mr. Frank called.

"You're welcome, Uncle Frank," Jess called, turning to Mrs. Isabella. "How was work today?" he asked politely.

She smiled. "Work," she laughed lightly. "But thanks for asking, sweetie. Well, I'm going to get cooking. Sammi, would you please stay for dinner? Your mom called and said she'd be home late tonight, and she can pick you up on her way home." She stood up and made her way to the kitchen.

I smiled. "That'd be a pleasure ma'am," I answered as I felt lips brush my temple. I looked at the clock on the cable box. It was only one o'clock. I looked up at Jess who was leaning down to look at me. "We did it Jess. We helped Alex." I put my head on his chest.

"Yeah we did. So, what are we going to talk about with Alex on Tuesday?" Jess asked. He put on his fake thinking face which involved his hand on his chin, a raised eyebrow, and a crinkled up face.

I laughed. "What's so funny?" Jess asked, snapping out of his fake thinking face. He smiled.

"I just love your fake thinking face." I giggled again.

"Awww," he pretended to pout. "It's supposed to look real."

I laughed and leaned my head on his shoulder. I yawned as Jess placed his cheek on the top of my head. Then, I fell asleep to the soothing sound of his breathing.

Chapter 9

"Ahhh!" I screamed as I ran. Ahead I saw a brick wall. I was cornered. I looked behind me to see if the man was still following me. He was. I turned back around to look at the wall almost tripping on a piece of concrete sticking out of the ground. I stopped, turned around and waited for the man to get closer. Two more seconds, I thought. Then, I jolted to my left just as he was about to grab me. I took off in the darkness behind him. As I got further and further away, I got closer and closer to something. It was big, red, and blocking my way. Another wall? How could it be there? This is where I just came from, I thought.

"There's nowhere to run. Nowhere to escape. No one to help you. Every last person you cared about is gone. You're alone!" the man whispered as he started running towards me again. His whispered words echoed along the walls, seeming to scream by the time they reached me.

The man had a thin black object in his hand. He aimed it at me and I heard a crack as I felt an agonizing pain tear through my left leg. I collapsed and hit my head off the wall and everything went fuzzy for a moment. I saw the man come into my eye range and hold the gun up to my face. He took something out of his pocket. It shimmered. Cowering. I watched as he turned his phone around and showed me a picture of someone beaten and bruised, bloody, tied in a chair, tape on their mouth, and unconscious. Both eyes were blackened like the person was wearing a mask. Blood flowed from their nose. It was dry and crusted. There was more blood squirming from their temple.

At first, I didn't recognize the face, but as seconds ticked by I realized who the body was. My heart shattered into a million pieces. It was Jess. I swallowed the lump in my throat and almost hurled from the searing pain in my leg and from my broken heart. There he was. My Jess, my match from God, beaten to death's door.

Then the man flicked his thumb to four other beaten and tattered bodies. My breath flew out of my lungs, leaving me gasping for air. Mom. Mrs. Isabella. Mr. Frank. Sarah...

The man put his phone back in his pocket and put both hands back on the gun. I shut my eyes tight and prayed to God it'd be quick. I prayed for Jess and his aunt and uncle. My mom and Sarah. I wished they'd die to be free. Then I heard a click.

"Aaaaahhhhh!" I screamed as my eyes flew open. I looked around, tears in my eyes, and sat up. *Ground yourself, Sam. Sight?* I saw bright blue walls hidden by shadows, a fish tank on the dresser and my betta fish swimming, and a peace sign comforter on the floor beside me. I took a deep breath. I was in my room.

Feeling nauseated, I grabbed my mini trash can from beside my bed and puked the contents of my stomach in it as the images flashed through my head like a slideshow.

"SAM!" my mom called. She darted in and knew, by the look on her face, what was wrong. She asked anyway. "Baby girl, what's wrong?" she asked, sitting next to me and wrapping me in a tight embrace. She picked up my blanket and laid it back over me.

"Mom...it was a nightmare," I choked out. "A man, he had a mask, chased me everywhere. He trapped me and shot me. He started saying I was alone. You were all gone. He showed me pictures of you, Jess, Mrs. Isabella, Mr. Frank, and Sarah. You were all... hurt. There was blood dripping off all of you. Then when he was done he shot me in the head. That's when I woke up. Mom..." I cried holding onto her tight, swallowing the bile trying to rise.

"Shhh, Sammi it's alright. That didn't happen. It's not real. Everyone's fine. And you very well know there isn't anyway anyone on this earth could keep Jesse from you. It's just the devil stealing your joy, sweetheart. Trying to pull you away. It's not true. You've got to be stronger than this." I went still and put a slight wall up.

Those phrases replayed over and over in my head.

That didn't happen...
You very well know...
You've got to be stronger...

I felt some more tears fall and my chest squeeze painfully as my dad popped into my head. *I miss you so much, Daddy. You always knew what to say.*

My mom began to hum a song my dad used to sing to me when I was younger.

"I love you," I added, still a little frightened.

"I love you, too. Try to get some rest. You have to meet Alex today," she said as she kissed my temple. "I love you, baby girl. Are you sure you're okay?" she asked as she reached the door.

"Yeah, I'll be okay." I said, forcing a smile. I felt my heart ache in my chest.

That didn't happen...
You very well know...
You've got to be stronger...

"Night. I love you. If you need anything I'm always right here." She walked out of my doorway as I said the same.

Then my phone rang. I looked at the screen. It was Jess. My heart leaped. I picked it up and pushed the green answer button. I held it up to my ear and said, "Hey, Jess." I coughed, clearing my throat, knowing my voice was still shaky.

"Hey, Sammi. I haven't really gone to sleep yet. Are you..." he paused. "Wait, another nightmare, huh?" he asked calmly, not wanting to set my tears off again.

"Yeah. It was a bad one," I said, feeling the back of my eyes heat up again.

"You wanna talk about it?" he asked, covering a yawn. I looked at my alarm clock next to my bed. It was three in the morning.

"I'm okay. You can go to sleep if you want." I hoped he would. "You sound exhausted and don't need me keeping you awake any longer." The picture of his battered appearance popped into my head, and I bit the inside of my cheek to keep from bawling. I quickly shook the picture out of my head and slid up a wall.

That didn't happen...
You very well know...
You've got to be stronger...

"I'm not sleeping either way if you're hurting. You don't wanna talk about it yet, huh?" he asked. *You know he's serious.*

I shook my head remembering he couldn't see that and said "No. Not really. Not tonight, anyway," I said, choking back tears.

"Well, whenever you're ready to talk, I'll always be here. And God's there for you to call on even if it's too personal you can't talk to me. Okay?" I could hear him smile.

The left side of my mouth slightly drew up, bringing my right side to join to become a full smile. Odd since I was still deathly terrified. "Thanks. Would you mind praying with me?" I asked, still shaky. I didn't think I could focus on anything but that horrifying dream.

"Of course not. Close your eyes. Dear God, we come before you this morning to lay our fears down on You. Please give Sammi the peace of mind, heart, and soul. Please fill her with the joy that was stolen from her. Purify her mind so she may be free from that demonic nightmare grasp that has been breaking her down from the inside for so long. I pray that she may be able to sleep peacefully tonight and be able to continue making the difference for You. We know You are always here. Please be with Sammi as she sleeps through these nightmares and give her the strength to say enough is enough. To stand up to the evil trying to live inside herself. I pray You also let her know I am always here and willing to listen. We give You all the honor and praise. In the name of Jesus, Amen."

"Amen," I repeated. "Thanks, Jess. I really appreciate it." I said, wiping away some stray tears that had fallen during his prayer.

"You're welcome. Wipe those tears away and send me a picture of your beautiful smile I fell in love with?" I could hear the corner of his lips lift into a grin as he spoke.

I giggled a bit and smiled. I took the phone off my ear and took a picture of my gross half smile. I put the phone back to my ear and said, "I just sent one."

"There's that beautiful smile," he chuckled into his mouth piece, suppressing a yawn. I rolled my eyes and smiled. "Thank you, Jess. I feel a lot better now." I smiled, truly feeling a bit better.

"Good. Now try and get some rest. I'll pick you up at seven. Okay?" he asked.

"Okay. And thanks again. You really didn't have to sit up and talk to me when you're so wiped. But I appreciate it."

"Yes I did. I never want to see you hurting, especially if I can help." The way he said it was like he just figured out he actually could read my mind.

"Well, thanks anyway. I'll see you soon. Bye, Jess. Love you," I said as I let a small yawn escape.

"Bye, Sammi. I love you, beautiful," he concluded as we hung up our phones. I laid down in my bed and stared at my ceiling. *Thank you God for giving me some peace of mind.* I thought. *I know you are mighty and all powerful.* I closed my eyes and drifted to sleep.

Chapter 10

"Hey Sam! Hey Jesse! Over here," Alex screamed, raising and waving a hand. He was sitting on a bench in the entrance of the park.

I looked at my phone. It was seven fifteen. He was early. "Hey Alex! How are you?" I asked as I gave him a small hug.

"I'm really good actually." He shook Jess's hand and smiled.

"That's great, Alex," I said, a little occupied. I pondered on my nightmare last night. I wondered what it meant.

That didn't happen...

You very well know...

You've got to be stronger...

"Hey Sammi, you alright?" someone asked, snapping me out of my dazed mind. I felt my hand get a light squeeze. I looked up to Jess. He had that 'I know what's wrong' face on. *Dumb mind reading abilities.*

"Yeah, I'm okay. So Alex, are you ready?" I asked, putting my dream in the back of my head.

"Yeah. I am," he said firmly. I smiled.

"Good. Where do you wanna go?" Jess asked.

"Are you guys hungry? I could buy us all some breakfast," he offered generously. He put his hands in his pockets.

"We can go to the fast food place. But I'm buying for you guys," Jess replied.

Alex smiled and shrugged. As we walked into the front doors, we stopped at the counter and saw a huge line. "Guys, I'll order the food on one tab and you can just pay me back later. Okay?" Alex asked.

"Okay," Jess and I said simultaneously.

"What do you guys want?" Alex asked.

"I'll have a number three," Jess replied.

"I'm okay, thank you though." I looked at the little plastic case they have for kid toys.

"Sam, hello," Alex said, waving a hand in my face. "Are you sure you're okay?"

"Yeah I'm fine. Sorry," I said as I snapped back to reality.

"Well you have to eat something," he encouraged.

"I'm okay. There isn't anything I'm hungry for," I lied. Insecurity hit me as I thought about eating and talking.

Jess squeezed my hand and led me to a booth as Alex ordered our food. He let me slide in first then slid in after me. "Hey, are you sure you're okay Sammi? You're sliding in and out a lot" he said, sounding concerned.

"This was the last place we went to together before my dad passed away." I pointed across the table at the left side of the seat. "My mom would sit there," I moved my hand to the right side, "and my dad there. I'd sit here and think about how happy they always were together."

"You remember those moments so well." Jess smiled.

"It's so weird. I can't remember some big things, but little moments I can easily. The first time I learned to hit a volleyball. The first day I met you and your," I stopped realizing what I almost said.

Jess smiled slightly and kissed the top of my head. "Me and my parents," he finished.

"Jess, they are not your parents. Blood doesn't make a family. Love does. But I can remember that day so clearly, the day my dad taught us how to ride our bikes, the first time we sang in church, the first time we prayed during service in church and a lady asked my mom if we could pray at a prayer breakfast." I continued running through the millions of memories I could see sprawled out in front of me.

"I remember that day. We were only four years old and you prayed better than most others could. You wore a purple, silk dress that had plastic, real looking flowers on the front, and white shoes that strapped on the side. You had your hair down, and a purple flower clip that kept your hair out of your face." He laughed. "I wore a small tux with a purple undershirt and clip-on tie. I escorted you up to the podium, where we stood on stools so we could reach the microphone." Jess chuckled a bit more.

"See? There's just certain things you can remember no matter your age or the time that passed." I smiled.

"I remember my blood mom and blood dad the first time they got me to sell drugs. They said if I didn't do it, I'd be locked in my room for a week with only water and a slice of bread." He looked out the window and tensed up.

I rested my hand on the side of his face, turned him back to look at me, and said, "I'm sorry. You shouldn't have to remember that. But is that why you couldn't sleep last night?" I felt so bad. *I lost one parent and felt like the world would end. What if I'd lost my mom too? And because of their actions?*

He leaned into my hand. "Yes. But it's okay. That was my past. You, Aunt Isabella, Uncle Frank, Sarah, and my friends, you guys are my future." He smiled and I pulled my hand away when we saw Alex coming our way with the tray of food. "Thanks man. Here," Jess said, handing him a ten for his food.

"No. At least if you have to pay me back, do it when we leave." He pushed Jess's hand away with a small nudge.

"Fine, but you're getting the money." Jess smiled, slipping the bill back in his pocket. He grabbed my hand.

"Let's pray over the food and get started with whatever Alex wants to start with," I jumped in. I grabbed onto Alex's hand as Jess did the same. "Okay. Dear Heavenly Father, we come before you today asking that you will please bless this food and free it from impurities. Please bless the hands that have prepared it. Please speak through Jess and I to help Alex become what You've made his future to be. We love you and give you all the honor and praise. In the name of Jesus, we pray, Amen," I concluded. Alex and Jess grabbed their sandwiches and opened them up. I watched as they each took a bite and smiled. "Okay Alex, so what do you wanna start with?"

He finished chewing and sat his breakfast sandwich down. "I wanna start with knowing how to forgive my mom I think." He looked from me to Jess and watched us closely.

"Okay. Well what do you wanna forgive her for?" Jess asked. We watched Alex hesitate and he added, "You don't have to tell us if you don't want to." He put his arm around me. I couldn't help but blush at the small, yet protective gesture.

    Alex took a deep breath. "No, it's okay. Um, for giving up after my father left and what she would do. She gave up on me and sat alone and depressed on the couch. She wouldn't talk to me unless she needed me to run out and get her alcohol or something. She always said 'someone is there'." He air quoted. "Give them the money and they'll go in and get it and give it back to me. She always said to bring it right back. One day she gave me one dollar instead of ten. I tried to tell her and she smacked me across the face so hard I fell into the tv. The screen cracked." I saw him swallow a huge lump in his throat and look down for a moment as his eyes started to glaze over.

    I put my hand on his, that laid on the table. I felt a lump grow in my stomach and sat up straighter knowing this story was only going to get worse. I felt Jess tighten his grip on me and I snuggled closer.

"She stood up and yelled at me for breaking the only thing that made her happy. She screamed it at me and I could tell she had been drinking. I rolled up into a tight ball afraid of what she would do. She grabbed my arms I had over my face and yanked them up out of the sockets. I cried so she punched me in my face and told me to shut up before someone heard I couldn't stop crying so she kept punching and kicking me until police rushed in and told my mother to freeze. They handcuffed her and locked her away for child abuse and neglect. I've been in the system since.

"Because of her giving up, I ended up in the hospital for a year. They had to fix the broken bones and had to get me to a healthy weight. I was starved. The only thing I ate was what I stole. I had surgeries and x-rays. So many X-rays and medicines and bright flashing lights and surgical masks..." he trailed off and looked out the window. He kept his focus there as he leaned back in the booth seat. "I was put in a psych ward because they were worried about my mental stability. That's where it came out that she had been," he paused and took a deep breath and whispered, "touching me since I was young." I went still as a statue and stopped breathing. *Don't go there, Sam. Just don't.* I put up as many barricades as I could in my head.

"I got put in a home at 12 years old. I've been waiting to be adopted but sadly never did. And no one ever wants a teenager. I just thought if I could meet a nice woman that could be my mom, I could forgive women in general," Alex stopped and looked at me and Jess' expressions with tears in his eyes. Jess's eyes were moist with tears that he wouldn't let fall. He always felt he had to be Mr. Strong.

Me, I probably looked like a wreck. I felt thousands of tears slide throughout his whole story. "Alex, I'm so sorry. Even after knowing what happened to Jess and hearing that, I still just can't believe how someone, who brought a child into the world, could be so vicious and evil to them. I'm so sorry for both of you. I wish neither of you had to live through what you did. But you should talk to Jess and let him answer questions since he knows more about the situation. Maybe you can even help each other." I looked at Alex who nodded and looked at Jess who kissed my head. I wrapped my arms around Jess's middle and prepared to listen to what was coming.

"I'm sorry, too. I wish you didn't have to live through that either. Since you trusted me, I'll trust you with my past." Jess spoke slowly and calmly. He took a deep breath, but I heard his heart beating rapidly. "My mom was fifteen when she had me. So was my father. He was in a gang. They made me sell drugs and steal from others. They would always threaten to lock me in my room for who knew how long. One time I actually stayed in my room for two weeks because my parents forgot about me. I had to crawl out of the two-story window and drink water from the hose and eat things I had to take, too. I always came back afraid of what they'd do if they found me trying to run away," he stopped. I felt him tighten his grip around me and clear his throat. I kept my gaze at the table trying to ground myself. A light grey table with a darker grey static pattern. *Count sections of specks, Sam. See any shapes?*

"Wow. So I'm not the only one. But, if you don't mind me asking, how'd you get away?" Alex questioned. I continued to stare at the table trying to force myself to listen. My heart ached and I wanted to disappear so badly. How could parents do such things?

"When I was seven, my aunt and uncle walked in on them beating me up pretty bad after they had gotten drunk. My uncle snatched me away from them and ran out the door behind my aunt. We got in the car and drove away quickly with my aunt holding me. She was rocking me." I heard Jess swallow. "I remember trying to hold her tightly and crying because I couldn't hang on. The bones in my arms were sticking out. I couldn't talk or see and my face hurt so bad. Eventually I passed out. They took me to a hospital and I was in there for about just as long as you. Surgeries, swelling in the brain, broken bones..." he trailed off. "Police asked me questions and told me everything would be okay. They arrested my mom and dad, locked them in jail. They got eight to fifteen years minimum," he said, trying to hide his emotions. "They got out this past Christmas for good behavior." Jess rocked his sandwich around in his hand before setting it back down and hugging me a bit tighter.

I shook my head and started breathing heavily. I couldn't even imagine the horrifying pain they were both admitting. My heart and body hurt, and I had to think of something quick. "Hey guys, can I make a phone call real fast?" I asked, needing to get away.

"Sure," they both said. Jess stood up and let me slide out. He kissed my cheek and watched me pull out my phone and walk outside. *Don't you cry, Sam. Stop being a baby. It isn't like it happened to you. Quit being a baby.*

I paced up and down the sidewalk trying to think of a way to help Alex. I scrolled through my contacts for no reason, when I ran across my mom. Then it hit me. I clicked on her contact and pressed the green call button. It rang once, then twice, then, "Hey, baby girl. Everything okay?"

"Yeah mom. Um I actually need to ask you a question. Remember when you and Daddy helped Aunt Daniella and her husband become foster parents?" I waited for her to respond.

"Yeah, I do."

"Well I'm with Alex right now and he was in the same situation as Jess except slightly different. He got put into the system and still is. All he wants is a home and a true family. I was wondering if maybe you could talk to Aunt Daniella about being able to foster him for a little while. I know it's a lot to ask, but," I stopped as my mother began to speak.

"When you get home, we'll get her and Derek and go to his group home and check it out. All of us. Okay?" she answered.

"Thank you, Momma! I love you so much!" I said into the mouthpiece.

"No problem, baby girl. I can't promise anything, but if you feel that's what he needs we'll check it out, Okay?"

"Okay. I love you! Bye." I said ecstatic.

"I love you, too. Be safe. Bye," she said as she hung up.

I walked back into the building and stopped behind Jess and heard him just as he said, "I know it feels impossible to have a real family again. But a wise, beautiful girl always tells me that blood doesn't make a family. Love does." My heart melted.

Alex, acknowledging my presence, smiled and asked, "Would that girl happen to be Sam?" His eyes flicked to mine and I smiled.

"She's a smart girl. She always tells me that when I'm feeling sad about my past. She makes me remember that it was my past. She's my future and helping her accomplish all the things she wants to in life." He stopped and looked at Alex's cheeky smile. He sighed and shook his head.

Knowing he was about to turn his head to look at me, I threw my arms around him from behind. "You're so sweet. Thank you," I said with a huge smile.

"Well it's true," he said, turning to kiss my lips. "Someone seems a lot happier now."

I looked at Alex and smiled even bigger. "Well it may be because of what you said." I giggled as he let me sit back down. Trying to keep my excitement contained, I reminded myself this is just an idea.

Chapter 11

"So we'll meet on Thursday. Okay?" I asked Alex as he walked to his group home.

"Okay, thanks!" he called.

"So spill it. Why were you so happy in there?" Jess asked me. I looked to the right and made sure Alex couldn't hear me. He walked into the group home and shut the door.

"Well for one, what you said about me being your future and helping change things with God's help. Two, he snuck your money back in your pocket without you noticing and asked me not to tell." I giggled as Jess reached in his back pocket. Sure enough, his ten was there.

"Wow. He's good," Jess admitted and grinned. "What else?" he asked. Pulling me close.

"I talked to my mom on the phone about my Aunt Daniella and Uncle Derek possibly fostering Alex." I quickly added, "Don't tell anyone." I put a finger to my lips.

Jess kissed my head and grabbed my hand as we started walking. "My lips are sealed. But how did you come up with that?" he asked, raising an eyebrow at me.

We looked both ways and crossed the street onto my block. I nudged my shoulders. "Those stories were just awful for me to hear. Some of the stories you told I've never even heard before," I added.

"Yeah, it's cause it's the first time I've told anyone some of those stories." His grasp tightened on my hand as a group of guys walked past us. I tensed and moved closer to Jess. They looked our way, but didn't bother us.

"Aw. I'm really sorry about all that. I just can't believe someone could be so cruel. Let alone to a child. When you were in the hospital that year, my dad told me you were sick. When I came to visit, you never told me anything." I looked up to my porch a couple houses away where my mom, aunt and uncle were all sitting, waiting for us. "Whenever you're willing to tell some of those, I'll be here. No matter how they upset me or you. It will be different when it's just us. I'm here to listen," I added just as we got to my porch.

"Thank you," Jess added quickly. "Hello, Mrs. Daniella, Mr. Derek, Mrs. Lisa." He nodded to each person as he said their name.

"Hello, Jesse. Samantha," Uncle Derek stated. "We hear you have an idea of a nice young man, who wants a good home. Should we go meet him?" he asked, probably thrilled with the thought of finally getting the chance at a son.

"I'll take us all down now," my mom put in. We all walked to the van as Jess and I hopped in the back, Uncle Derek was in the middle, Aunt Daniella in the passenger's seat, and my mom driving.

"It's the one on Jordan Street," Jess added as we all put our seatbelts on.

As we pulled away from the shrivel of concrete that was the curb, the adults started a conversation. I sat behind Uncle Derek and Jess sat right next to me. "I almost forgot. Are you still okay about this morning?" he asked in a hushed tone. He wrapped his arm around my shoulders.

"Um...is it still okay if I talk about it?" I asked, still a little fearful of going to sleep again. He chuckled a bit as if he were surprised by my question. "Of course you can, Sammi." I took a breath. I told him about the entire nightmare. The masked man, how he was saying I was alone, shooting me in the leg, and all. Then I got to the part about the five bodies. Jess tightened his grip on me as he saw tears drift down my face as I told him that I couldn't recognize the first body. Then after what seemed like forever I realized. Then I talked about the pictures of Mr. Frank, Mrs. Isabella, my mom, and Sarah. As I finished the story by waking up in my bedroom after being shot, I put my head on his shoulders and wiped away my tears.

"Wow. Sammi, that was a crazy dream. Did you see who the man was?" he asked me softly.

"No. He had a black hat with two eye holes and a mouth hole," I informed him.

"I'm so sorry, Sammi. I wish I could've been there. But I promise I'm good. I'm okay. We all are." He kissed the top of my head.

"I know. Thanks. It just hurt me to see the people I love so much, hurt and beaten, I didn't even know who they were. I mean you were black and blue, green and yellow, with blood coming from your hair, mouth, and nose, and tape on your mouth. You were tied to a chair and unconscious. Even if you weren't, you probably couldn't speak or open your eyes anyway. I didn't even know who you were." I squeaked out quietly, trying to stop the tears from sliding again.

"Pray. That's all you can do to get that peace. And if you can't, call me. You know I'm always here," he continued, speaking softly. "Also know that nobody, but God himself, could keep me away from you, no matter the beating I get." He pecked my lips softly and looked into my eyes. So much safety sat in those hazel eyes.

I wiped my eyes and snuggled into him closer. "Thanks, Jess," I said, feeling enormously better. We felt the car jerk to a stop and looked out the window. We saw kids running, playing, and laughing. Living life freely and as happy as they can. There were kids of all ages.

We all crawled out of the van and walked up onto the curb. I saw a little boy, about nine years old sitting alone. I called to everyone, "Hey guys, I'll meet you inside."

"Me, too," Jess added. "What are you up to, Sammi?"

I nodded to the little boy. I grabbed a piece of stray chalk on the ground and drew a hopscotch court to twelve as best as I could on these messed up sidewalks. I watched Jess sit on the side of the steps and watch me carefully.

I walked over to the little boy and leaned down next to him. "Hello," I said gently. "I'm Samantha. But if you like, you can call me Sammi or Sam." I watched as the little boy continued to stare at the ground. "What's your name?" I asked.

He just looked at me. I saw pain in his eyes. Like Alex the first day we met him. He whispered, "It doesn't matter. You don't actually care." He looked back at the ground. I saw a small tear fall to the dirt underneath him. He must have known too because he quickly pushed dirt over it using the toe of his shoe.

I frowned and said, "That's not true. I saw you being all alone and thought I could make a new friend." I smiled kindly.

The young boy studied my face hard. *What have you been through?* "Are you telling the truth? Or just lying to me?" he interrogated.

I stuck out my hand for him to shake. "I am Sammi or Sam. Whichever is fine and I will not lie to you."

He looked at my face then my hand. He slowly lifted his and shook my hand. "I'm Brent. I'm seven."

"Wow, you look older than seven. I thought you were nine," I complimented.

I saw him let go a small smile. "Really? I can't wait to be nine! It's one year before ten. Then I get a one in front of my age." He held up his index finger as one.

"Really? That will be neat. I was so excited for my tenth birthday. I'm almost seventeen now. So if I didn't have my tenth birthday I'd only be seven." I made a surprised face. "I'd be the same age as you," I smiled as I watched him giggle slightly. "You wanna play a game with me?" I asked Brent.

"Sure but I only know a few," he informed me.

My heart tugged lightly. "I know plenty. You know how to play hopscotch?" I asked, taking his hand as we stood up. I looked down at him.

"Is that the game where you toss a rock, and whatever number, you jump on one leg then two legs, then one again?" he asked.

"Yes sir, but you only toss the rocks on the court, and only whenever someone older's here to watch," I replied as I led him to my hopscotch course.

"Okay," he replied sweetly. "I love that game. Can I go first?" he asked, picking up a small pebble.

"Of course you can. Ready...go!" I said as he tossed his pebble. He landed on 3 and hopped to get it and hopped back.

"Your turn!" he said. "Ready...set...go!" he hollered. I tossed mine to a seven. I hopped up to get it. I realized the seven was a one block so I had to lean down on one foot and get it while balancing on cracked, uneven concrete. It didn't work out. I almost fell and put my other foot down. Brent started laughing and pumping his fist in the air. "I win!" he called. He giggled as I walked back over to him.

I kneeled down, smiled and gave him a high five. "Wayta go! You're really good at this game!" I congratulated him.

"Kids! It's time for dinner!" a lady hollered from the doorway. She held the door open as the young kids raced inside.

All the kids ran into the building. "Will you come back and play with me again?" Brent asked.

"Of course. Now, don't be the last to get something to eat. Bye, Brent!" I called as he ran up the steps.

"Bye, Sam!" he repeated. Then he disappeared through the doorway.

"Wow, Sammi. You've got such skills when it comes to getting people to open up," Jess said walking back over to me.

I jumped, forgetting he was still there. "He was alone and sad. I just did what anyone would have done." I shrugged my shoulders as we walked towards the entrance.

"You're wrong. Not any normal person would do that, Sammi." He grabbed my hand as we walked up the steps.

"Thanks," I said, feeling embarrassed.

"No really," he continued, stopping me. He took both of my hands so I was facing him. "You may not like the stories that go along with these kids and even me, but you can definitely gain our trust like nothing I've seen from *just anybody*," he emphasized.

"I just don't like to see people like that. Everyone's a star in God's eyes, so why should you be alone because of mistakes someone else made?" I questioned.

He pulled me close, wrapped his arms around my waist, and kissed me softly. "I love you."

"I love you." I laid my head in the crook of his neck and shut everything out. I just wanted this moment to last.

....

We walked into the building and I looked around. There were tons of chairs and couches sprawled across the huge room. All of them were torn with the stuffing falling out. Four old TVs all spread out. There were old ping-pong and foosball tables. There were cracks in the walls and stains on the blue wall paper. We walked up to the reception desk to the right and watched as the lady from before put down her phone. "Can I help you?" she asked calmly.

"Hello ma'am. My mother, Lisa Addams, and my Uncle Derek McCartney and Aunt Daniella McCartney came to speak to Alex Daniels," I informed.

"Oh, why yes. They went through that door and made the second left," she said as she pointed across the room to a door.

"Thank you," I appreciated. I turned on my heel and began to walk away.

"Oh and young lady!" she called after me. I turned around to face her. "May I ask what both of your names are?" she asked.

"I am Sammi Addams and this is Jesse Jackson."

"Yes, that's what I thought. You are the two teens from the park. I was wondering if you two would like to start coming by during the summer and volunteering here? I saw what you did for Brent. He hasn't smiled and laughed like that for the year he's been here. Thank you"

I smiled and looked at Jess who nodded. "We'd love to." I said excitedly.

The lady gave a smile that could melt an entire glacier. "Thank you so much. It will be nice for these kids to be around the two of you. Whenever you have the time, stop by. Please," she encouraged. She waved us along.

"Yes, ma'am. We will do that," Jess answered politely and nodded to her as we walked away.

"See? Not just any ordinary person could do that." He smiled as we walked through the first door. I gasped as we saw a huge hallway. On the right was, what looked like, a huge dining room filled with tables and kids like a school cafeteria. I saw Brent who waved at me and looked a lot happier than before. I smiled as I saw he was sitting with other kids. I waved back as we passed the entrance and made our way to the second door on the left.

Jess opened the door for me and let me walk inside, then followed after. We walked into a room that looked like a conference room. A long table, and one chair on the inside, four chairs on the other side. Except no one was in the chairs. Aunt Daniella and Uncle Derek were hugging Alex beside the table and crying. My mom was back, watching the scene, smiling to herself.

 I watched Alex closely. He hung onto my aunt and uncle for dear life. He was in tears, but his face was lit up so bright. "Thank you!" he kept repeating.

 Aunt Daniella repeated, "You're welcome! I hope you'll be happy with us."

 I couldn't help but smile. Alex was getting what he wanted all along. Maybe this would make it a little easier to forgive his mother. To forgive himself for the guilt he felt. Like he didn't deserve happiness.

 "Can Sam pray?" he asked all of us, still weeping.

 "Sure," I said, taken off guard. "I'd love to, Alex. Ready?" I asked as everyone nodded. The hand Jesse wasn't holding, I stretched out to my mom. I began as I felt her grab my hand and sandwich it between hers. "Dear Heavenly and Gracious God, we come before You today thanking You for Alex and the gift of his friendship. We thank You for my aunt and uncle's parental willingness to take Alex into their home and to give him a better life. Thank You for showing him You are almighty and all powerful. That his life rests in Your hands, Father God. That You do love him and care for him. That you want what's best for him. We thank You for Alex's willingness to learn about you. We love You, praise You, and give You all the honor and glory. In Your name, Amen," I finished. I opened my eyes and looked around. My aunt and uncle still had Alex in a tight embrace.

"Amen," everyone repeated. My mom squeezed my hand. She let go and went to pat Aunt Daniella on the back. Jess picked me up in a hug. I smiled as my feet left the ground and he kissed my cheek. I hugged him tightly, feeling my heart mend. I held him tight as we watched the scene before us. Even though Alex, just like Jess, had a hard past, God never abandoned him. He would be okay.

Chapter 12

We felt the car swerve to a stop as we pulled in front of Lé Café. My mom parked and we all climbed out of the van. My mom, Jess, and I took the lead and went to find a table, since Aunt Daniella, Uncle Derek, and Alex hadn't finished their hug.

Jess, my mom and I sat at a high, six person table. There were six chairs, clumped in groups of three on either side. It felt weird for my feet to not touch the floor. I held onto Jess's hand, so thrilled to have a new cousin. This is his welcome to the family dinner.

"Sammi, my baby girl," my mom began. "You too, Jess." She nodded to Alex, my aunt, and uncle on the opposite side of the window. "Look at what you two have done. Look how happy you've made all three of them. You both are truly my blessings. Thank you," she said, rubbing each of our hands.

"Thanks, Mrs. Lisa. But this one was all Sammi. I was talking with Alex about his past. Sam, being the compassionate person she is, couldn't listen to some of the stories we shared, and went outside and came up with the idea. She even helped a little boy named Brent at the group home. The lady at the front desk asked us to start volunteering there," Jess informed. He put his arm around me and smiled down at me. I looked down feeling a bit awkward. *Light blue table with black outlining.*

    My mom's face didn't change. "I'm not surprised. There is not one person that doesn't pass me and say 'you should be so proud'. I am," she added. "Of both of you. You both had to deal with things no kids should ever have to deal with. You truly are an amazing pair that God put here together for a reason." She tightened her grip on our hands. She let a tear slide.

    "Thank you, mom," I said genuinely.

    "Thank you, Ms. Lisa," Jess added.

    My aunt and uncle sat down as Alex came over to Jess and I and threw his arms around both of us. "Thank you so much! I can't believe all of the things you two have done for me. Thanks to you, I know someone loves me, I have two new friends, now a new friend and a cousin, and now, I finally have a home. Thank you two so much," he finished squeezing us.

We both hugged him and rubbed his back separately. "You are so welcome. But don't thank me, thank God. He let us meet you. He let us take you to church. He gave me and my mom the idea to bring my aunt and uncle to you. He did this for you. He loves you, Alex. And so do we," I said meaning every word.

"I love you guys, too," he added. He took his arms from around us and walked to my mom and did the same, he thanked her as she said your welcome. Then he went to sit back down between my Aunt Daniella and Uncle Derek.

Jess put his arm back around me and kissed my cheek. I saw everyone watching us. I didn't know what would be next, but I hoped God would just keep using me.

···

"Welcome to your new home Alex!" my aunt hollered as we all exited the van.

"Wow!" Alex gasped. My Aunt Daniella and Uncle Derek's house is a three bedroom with a living room, a kitchen, a family game room, and two bathrooms. We also have a pool in the back we share. "I can't believe I'll be living here!" Alex said, staring up at the house. He ran his fingers along the wooden fence that surrounded both my yard and my aunt and uncle's yard. He watched as my Uncle Derek opened the fence and let him and my Aunt Daniella through.

"See you later, Alex!" Jess and I called, each waving a hand as Jess sneezed.

"Bless you, bye, and thank you!" he hollered as he entered his new home.

My mom, Jess, and I entered my house and all sat down at the kitchen table together.

"Wow. I feel so good," I said sitting down between my mom and Jess, who sneezed into his arm.

"Bless you and you should," my mom said with a yawn. She covered her mouth and I could tell she was exhausted.

"You sound tired, mom. You wanna go lay down?" I asked. She was probably still tired from waking up at three in the morning.

She thought about it, then said, "I may have to take you up on that. Behave and if you go somewhere, leave a note." She stood up, kissed both of our foreheads, and headed over to the steps. She paused as Jess sneezed again, and turned around to face us. "Bless you, and you two should be very proud of yourselves. I love you, both." Then she turned around and started up the steps.

"Yes ma'am, thank you, and I love you, too mom!" I said still jittery with excitement. Jess sneezed again.

"Bless you and I'll take that as I love you, too. The keys are on the table if Aunt Daniella and Uncle Derek wanna go anywhere," she called as her bedroom door shut and then she opened it. "We've got work today for a few hours." She sighed. "I'll be up in an hour or two." She shut her door again.

"Wow, what a day." Jess sneezed into his arm again.

"Bless you. Are you allergic to me, Jess?" I asked him. "You've been sneezing for the last couple of hours."

He smiled and stuck his tongue out at me. "Very funny. Other than pollen, not allergic to anything that I know of," he shrugged, sneezing again.

I felt his head. "Did you take allergy medicine this morning?" I asked him, watching closely.

"Well that might explain it," he said, giving a small shake of his head. "I ran out. And no wonder I'm sneezing," he said, taking his phone out.

"Whatcha doing?" I asked, trying to see.

"Checking the weather report. The pollen count has been through the roof for about two hours now. That explains a-CHEW!" he sneezed again.

"Maybe we should go to the store and get you some and bless you," I recommended.

"Maybe you're right," he laughed.

"Let's go. Just let me write my mom a note first," I said just as the doorbell rang.

"I'll get it," Jess offered. He got up from the table and went to look through the peephole. "Hey, it's your cuz," Jess said, opening the door for Alex. "Hey, what's up

Alex?" Jess asked Alex, giving Alex a weird half-high-five-half-hug thing all men do.

"Mr. Derek and his wife have to go to work and wanted to know if you guys could go shopping with me. Something about buying some clothes and some new shoes," he said, pulling out some cash.

"Sure we can. We have to pick up some allergy medicine for Jess anyway," I said as Jess sneezed yet again, only confirming my point.

"Bless you. Thanks. I tried to convince them I had enough and I didn't need a lot. They said to take you guys to make sure I get more than enough." He added, "If I went alone, I'd come back with like ten dollars less than I left with and one pair of pants." He laughed slightly.

"Well let's go," I said walking over to the steps. "Hey mom, we're taking Alex to the mall. Love you!" I called.

"Love you, too. Be careful!" she replied.

"Alright. Let's roll," Jess said, sneezing again.

"Yeah, right down to the store to get you some allergy medicine!" I joked. "Bless you, Jess."

"Thank you," he said, holding the door open for Alex and I. He kissed my cheek as I walked past and grabbed my hand after shutting the door.

Chapter 13

"Wow! I've never been in the mall before," Alex said. I was pretty sure his eyes were gonna fall out of his head. He marveled at the huge fountain in the middle of the mall. It had escalators leading up to all four floors. There was a glass sunroof, and hundreds of stores occupying the space.

"Well, where do you wanna start?" Jess asked. He gave my hand a small squeeze as he smiled and watched Alex turn in a complete circle.

"Uhh...no clue at all. What stores do you shop at?" he asked, looking at Jess again. He switched his weight from one foot to the next. .

"I like this store. They have cool clothes and they're extremely cheap." Jess nodded at a store behind him and sneezed. He turned his head and looked at the window. "And they're having a summer sale," he added, acknowledging the sign in the window.

"Bless you. Let's go," Alex said as we made our way to the store. It was a perfect time to shop at the mall. Only a few groups of teens were there with some of their parents or older siblings. Not crowded at all.

We walked into it just in time to be blasted by harsh music. People just had to put speakers right by the door. "You'll just have to tune out the music until we get away from the door. You can't hear it once we get a little farther into the store," Jess educated. I looked down at the checkered floor. I could see my reflection.

"Well, where do I start?" Alex asked, eyes bulging like a child's in a candy store. He turned around three-hundred and sixty degrees.

Jess pointed towards the flannels and sneezed. "I saw you slow down when you ran your eyes past those," he chuckled. "You wanna start there?" He asked.

"Bless you, again, and sure. Will you help me with all of this? I've never actually done this before." Alex looked down embarrassed. His cheeks heated up.

I put my hand on his shoulder. "You don't have to be embarrassed around us, Alex. You're my cousin," I said softly and genuinely.

Alex picked his head up with a smile on his face. He again grabbed me in a hug. I returned it and kissed his cheek. "Welcome to the family, Alex." I smiled as he picked me up off the ground.

"Thank you so much. I know I keep saying it, but thank you so much. I'll never be able to repay you," he added. He set me down and turned to Jess. "Both of you, thank you." He turned around and looked at the rack behind him. He ran his fingers over the hangers.

"I'll be over there till you guys need some help," I said pointing to the female side of the store.

"Okay," Alex said simply.

"Okay," Jess echoed and sneezed into his arm.

"Maybe I should go to the store and get you that medicine first," I said with a small giggle. "I'll go get it now. I'll be back," I called while walking out of the store.

I looked down at the freshly waxed floors. I could still smell the fumes from the floor polish. I looked ahead at the small shop. It wasn't packed and the medicine aisle was right in the front, next to the checkout lines. I walked to it and looked for a small bottle of allergy medicine. I grabbed one and also grabbed a ninety-nine cent water bottle.

I walked to the checkout aisle and put the small bottle and water bottle in the clerk's hand. "Is that all?" the woman asked. She rang it up without even looking at me and put it in a small bag.

"Yes ma'am. That's all," I answered respectfully. I watched her. She looked exhausted. "Four seventy-five," she replied harshly.

I took the exact amount out of my wallet and set it in her outstretched hand. "Thank you, and have a wonderful day," I finished as I began to walk away.

"Yeah, yeah," she snarled under her breath, keeping her head down.

I turned the direction back to the store the boys were in and began to retrace my steps. Then, something caught my eye. It was a small cart. A normal, average, everyday cart. But what was unique about it was the objects that sprawled out on the flat surface. They were beautiful ornaments in tons of different shapes and relevant meanings on a plaque underneath the art. There were shapes, words, people, and animals. All wonderfully sculpted out of fine glass. At the bottom were small buttons you could push, and a random colored light would shine through the glass and cast a gorgeous luminescent glow.

    One ornament stood out from all the others, though. It was a clear glass cross. The little plaque underneath it said, "Do not let anyone look down on you because you are young. Instead set an example for the believers in speech, in faith, in love, in conduct, and in purity". That is one of my absolute favorite scriptures. I picked it up carefully to admire it some more. I noticed a small figure attached to the cross. It was a dove. Then a child with a teddy bear stood in front of the cross, looking up at it.

    I thought about buying it. I looked at the price tag on a little cardboard stand right in front of where the sculpture sat. I shook my head and set it back down. It was fifty dollars. I didn't have fifty dollars to spend. I walked through the entrance of the store quickly to avoid the music. I looked for Alex and Jess. I saw Jess over by a rack by the changing room. I made my way over to him. Alex came out in the same clothing he had on when we first came in.

"I'll get these ones," he said, hanging the other ones back up on the rack. A plaid light and dark red one, blue and green one, orange and red one, black and yellow one, and a turquoise and a dark blue one were left wrapped over his arm.

Alex led the way up to the checkout section and set his shirts on the counter. "Is that all for ya today, hun?" a lady asked politely with a bright smile. Alex only nodded. He kept his eyes down on the counter. The woman handed him the bag. He took it and said thank you softly.

"You are very welcome. Hey, ya ever come back here, tell them Janie Bell sent ya, and you'll get the employee discount for the rest of the summer. Not just anyone can get that," she informed us.

Alex lifted his head and smiled. "Th-thank you," he stuttered.

"No problem, dumplin. Ya mind if I take ya name with the other counter people's choices?" she asked. "You can just give me ya name and we'll put it back here where only we'll see it." She winked.

"Uhh, it's Daniel Alexander," he replied.

"Okay, so say Janie Bell, and ya name." She looked back at us. "Oh my stars. Y'all are Sam Addams and Jesse Jackson, ain't y'all?" she asked, coming out from around the counters.

"Yes ma'am. We are," Jess admitted. I watched him smile and did the same.

She gave us both a huge hug and smile. "Y'all are some mighty fine kids. Y'all are really making a difference. I think ya know my nephew, Alejandro. He's in the choir wit y'all at church."

"Oh. Yes. He's one of my best friends," I said, returning the smile.

"Oh that's good," she added, returning behind her counter. "Bye! It was nice to meet y'all," she called.

"Nice to meet you too!" I called as Jess led the way out of the store.

"Do you guys wanna go up to the food court so Jess can take his allergy medicine, and we can get some type of desert?" I asked. I could really go for a smoothie.

Alex nodded his head. "I really want to buy a Cherry Freeze," he said, putting his money in his pocket, and receipt in the bag.

"I'm up for it. I'm pretty sure I sneezed my brain out about an hour or so ago. So," Jess added, sneezing into his arm again. "Yep, just as I thought."

"What?" Alex asked as we began to walk toward the glass elevator. I smiled, knowing it was going to be something silly.

"No brain left to sneeze," he finished. He smiled as Alex and I both giggled.

We got to the elevators and hopped on. I saw a man walking towards us just as the doors began to shut. I quickly held the doors open for the man to get on.

"Why thank you, young lady," he said sincerely. He moved off to the opposite side of the elevator.

"Of course." I said, pushing the four button to go up to the fourth floor. I looked at the man kindly. I've seen this man before. His clothes. It was all so familiar. I had seen him before. I just didn't know where. "I'm sorry sir, but have we met before?" I asked, thinking hard.

"I don't believe so. Wait, you're the girl that walked past my tent last Tuesday, I think it was. Black coat with tears in her eyes?" he answered, keeping his head down.

"Oh. I'm so sorry. Would you like me to buy you some lunch?" I asked genuinely.

"No no. You don't have to do that," he said, softening up a bit, but still keeping his head down.

"I know I don't have to, but I want to. Please," I begged. I felt Jess's hand squeeze mine. I looked up at him and he was smiling down at me.

"Yeah. Please let us buy you lunch. You've helped us a lot," Jess coaxed. I looked at Alex who was eyeing the guy carefully.

"Wow, really?" the man asked looking up. He had a surprised look on his face. It hurt my heart.

"Yes," Jess said. "It'd be a pleasure to buy you lunch."

The elevator door opened to our floor and we stepped out. The man followed us to a table for six. Jess, Alex, and I sat on one side, the man on the other.

I sat between Alex and Jess. "Is there anything you want to eat?" I asked.

"Uh, just a small amount of water would be fine. Thank you." He sat back in his seat quietly.

I handed Jess the bag with his medicine and the water to him. He handed me a twenty and a ten. "I will go get everyone something and will be back." I stood from the table, let go of Jess's hand, and kissed his cheek. I pulled away slowly as I whispered, "Would you be okay if Alex came with me?" I asked quietly. He nodded.

Alex, because you know everyone can read my mind, stood up and said, "I'll help you."

We walked over to a small little ordering counter. I ordered two tropical very berry smoothies, a cherry Freeze, and a burger meal with water. We waited off to the side as our food was being made fresh. "Wow Sam. You never stop thinking of others, huh?" Alex asked with a small smile. I looked at the huge food court, with its hundreds of red tables, and variety of food counters. It's high ceilings and a skylight view. "Well, I just don't understand how society could make people less important than other people." I shook my head. "The key word there is people. I just want everyone to be happy and taken care of," I said looking at him. "I try to help everyone I can."

    His smile just got bigger. "Before I met you and Jesse," he began, "I didn't think there was anyone who cared about anyone. When any decisions are being made, all you hear is 'As long as it don't affect me, I'm fine.'" Alex sat down on his heels, stood back up, and leaned on the wall. "Well what if it affects your friends, your parents, your kids, their kids? I thought everyone was selfish and no one cared about anyone else. Then I met you two." He smiled.

"Order number seventeen is ready!" a lady called. I looked at our receipt and we both walked over to grab our stuff. Alex took the tray of the man's food and his Freeze. I carried the smoothies.

We walked over and paused as Jess was praying with the man. I watched as the man had tears escaping from his eyes. He was silent. Listening to Jess's every word. "Amen," Jess said, opening his eyes to look at the man.

"Amen," the man echoed. He stood up and waited for Jess to do the same. Then he gave him one of those half hug things. "Thank you, kid. I haven't experienced such kindness in a long time. It means so much to know that you youngsters care about an old man who lost his mind."

Jess patted his back. "Of course we care. Just because we are young doesn't mean we don't care. After my girlfriend saw you last week, she came to my house devastated. She was so disappointed. You are actually one of the reasons that she wanted to make a change," Jess said.

He pulled away from Jess quickly. "That's where I know you two from. You two and other teens are in the paper. You guys cleaned the park?" The man's eyes lit up.

"That's us. But before you go, please remember no one can push you that far. If you've got God, it'll get better. Sometimes all you can do is rest until you can fight again. God's okay with that. Just don't give up." Jess sat back down and realized we were behind him. Alex and I sat down. I kissed Jess's cheek and handed him his smoothie. Jess put his arm around my shoulders and took a sip.

I watched him and the man as the man said, "Excuse me kids but I must be off. I have someone I have to call. Thank you so much for your kindness." He stood up.

"Wait!" I called. "Take your meal with you." I pointed to the tray.

He looked at me, to Alex, then to the tray. "R-really?" he asked. I saw a tear faintly fall from his eye.

"Yes. Take it," Alex said. "It's all yours," he added. He handed the tray full of boxed food to the man.

The man reached out a shaky hand and took the tray. "Thank you, kids. Thank you," he said, turning away as he wiped a tear.

"No problem," Jesse said. "Good luck! God hasn't forgotten the plans he has for you." With another thank you, the man was on his way.

We watched him leave and turned to Jess. "What happened?" Alex asked.

"He told me his story. I took my allergy medicine and he asked if I was addicted to prescription drugs. I said no. He said that was good. He ruined his life that way." Jess looked in the direction the man walked to.

Alex exhaled heavily. "Wow."

"Yeah. He said he got hooked on them when he was sixteen. He got a bad concussion and they prescribed him a narc pain killer. When he got married, he used money from his and his wife's savings to buy them. When she found out, she divorced him and kicked him out. She said she loved him with all she had, but he couldn't come back until he was done with the drugs. He said he's been done with them for years now, but was afraid to call. That's what he meant by, 'I got someone to call,'" Jess finished.

"That's really sad," I admitted, taking a drink of my smoothie. "Is that why you were praying with him?" I asked, looking at Jess.

"Uh, no. He was so hungry and was so tired of fighting his way that he was gonna do something to get him sent to jail. He said at least there's three meals a day, showers, and a place to sleep," Jess paused. He shook his head and looked through the food court in the direction the man left.

"Oh wow," Alex said. "He wanted to go to jail?" Alex shook his head.

Chapter 14

"This is a lot of stuff. I really don't need all of this," Alex said, bringing his bags into my house for now. Alex didn't have a key to his house yet.

"They texted me after lunch and said, 'Get him more than enough,'" Jess recalled.

"We passed that boat," Alex laughed, setting his five bags of clothes and two bags of shoes down.

"Well anyway, what do you guys wanna do?" I asked just as Jess's phone rang. I watched him take his phone out, push the green answer button, and put it to his ear.

"Hey, Dom. What's up?" Jess said into the mouthpiece. A few seconds ticked by as Alex and I looked from each other to Jess. "Wait, what?" he asked. I heard a hint of surprise and worry in his voice. "Yeah we'll be there in fifteen minutes." He hung up the phone and looked at me. He looked uneasy. "We've gotta get to the hospital," he said, turning away from me and walking over to the door. He opened and waited for us to step out. I looked from Alex to

Jess. That hint of worry, nervousness, and surprise scared me. If Jess let it show in his voice like that, I don't even know what could be wrong.

Alex and I scurried to the door. Alex flew through it, I locked it, and led Jess out. He grabbed my hand as he started walking quickly, left, past my aunt and uncle's house. Alex walked quickly to the left of me. Jess close to my right.

I looked up at Jess to see if I could see a hint of anything from his face. Nope. Nothing. Just collected Jess. Not so much the calm, but collected nevertheless. "Jess, what's wrong?" I asked, my suspicions getting higher and higher.

"Uh, I'd rather not say until you see for yourself," he said, continuing to walk at the same pace, just barely looking at me. We got to a corner, looked both ways, and crossed the street. "All I will say is that someone got into a car accident," he said, shaking his head. He gave me a quick glance and a squeeze of my hand. I looked at Alex who just shrugged. He looked a little worried, too.

We continued to walk along the streets, navigating our way through the twist of plants that grow up through the aged, cracked concrete. We walked past a house with a little girl learning to ride a bike. She tipped over and scraped her knee and elbow. Then her dad came over, picked her up, and kissed her knee and elbow. He held her closely, whispering to her softly, encouraging her tiny cute little giggle to present itself.

I felt a small jab in my heart. My father did that to me and Jess when he taught us to ride a bicycle. I'm glad that little girl had a father who wasn't afraid to pick her up and make her feel better when she was hurt.

By the time I shimmied out of my thoughts, the little girl and her father were long gone. "Jess," I said softly.

"Yeah?" he asked as we turned a quick left around the corner.

"Did you see the little girl and her father?" I asked drifting back to some memories. "Yeah," he replied. "He reminds me of your dad." He gave my hand a small squeeze. "That's what I thought," I said, snapping back to reality.

We continued walking for another ten minutes and hooked a left. The hospital came into sight, and I started to worry about what was behind those walls waiting for us. As the doors separated and we approached the lobby desk, my heart started beating faster and faster. The knot in my stomach just got tighter to the point I was struggling to swallow. The clicking of the keyboard made my anxiety start to swell in my chest. "We are here to see the girl in the accident," Jess said to the receptionist. Then he whispered something to her.

The woman took a break from her typing, watched us for a moment, then gave a half smile. She seemed tired. Her eyes looked like they wished they could drift shut. "Up three floors in waiting room A." She gave a sad smile and pointed us in the direction of the elevators.

"Thank you," Alex replied. "Have a good day, ma'am." We advanced quickly on the doors off to our right. We climbed on and I pushed the button on the wall. I moved back to the rear of the elevator, between Alex and Jess.

    I felt the elevator slowly shift its way upward. I heard one ding. Then another. Then the last as the door separated for us to step through. I felt a squeeze in my hand. I peered up at Jess. He stepped out and pulled me off to the left.

    "Alex, there are some people our age up ahead. They're from school. You might know some of them." He nodded in the general direction of the waiting room.

    "Okay. I'll go introduce myself," he said, giving us a skeptical glance, then turning the direction Jess nodded.

    Jess moved his focus back on me, taking both of my hands. "Hey Sammi, you okay? You haven't said a word for a while." He spoke calmly. Exactly the way he would if I had just dreamt a nightmare, and he was on the phone with me.

    "Yeah, I'm okay. Just a little," I stopped. I didn't even know what I was. The feeling I had was a combination of fear, surprise, sadness, worry, and a stream of other emotions drifting through my brain. But whatever it was, there definitely wasn't only a little of it. "Jess, I know we are gonna be waiting for a while. So just promise me some things."

"Sure, Sammi. Anything," he expressed to me.

"Just please tell me it's not my... my mom." I looked down hoping I wouldn't hear the

deadly words.

"No no. It's not your mom, your aunt, uncle, my Uncle Frank, Aunt Isabella, or Sarah. Nobody related to us," he confirmed.

I took a deep breath partially relieved. I threw my arms around Jess and held him tightly. I don't know what I would have done if it had been my mom or my family member.

I felt Jess' arms encase me. A stray tear fell once again as the harsh reality hit me like a

sack of bricks. Who was in the accident then? I didn't want to know yet.

"It's someone from school. We saw her a few times in the last couple of weeks. She's really banged up," Jess informed. "We probably won't see her for a couple hours. Her parents are in there with her now. She just woke up from her third round of surgery. The doctor called her friends because she needs to be surrounded by people she knows."

"Why?" I asked, pulling away slowly. I looked into his eyes to see if I could read them. Of course I couldn't interpret anything at all.

"She's got a concussion and some memory loss. The doctors don't know what and how much of it she can remember. She remembers the simple stuff like how to eat and that type of stuff, but doesn't remember who her friends are, where she lives, and stuff like that," Jess continued.

I felt him squeeze my upper arms gently and gaze into my eyes. He watched me closely. Then brought me closer and kissed my forehead. He knew I was fighting my head.

I shook my head clean and pulled away. "A-a-a-anything else the d-doctor said?" I asked. I really hoped the stuttering was only that bad in my head. By the look on Jess's face, I could tell that's how it sounded in real life, too. I cleared my throat. "I mean did the doctor say anything else?" I took a deep breath.

Jess's eyes roamed from me, then to the waiting room. I knew he was keeping something from me. I was just too afraid to ask what 'it' was.

"I don't know anything else. That's all Dom told me." He grasped my hands. "Are you okay?" he asked genuinely.

"Y-y-yeah. I'm f-fine." Shoot. Gotta get that stuttering under control. Jess led me through the long white sterilized hall, in the direction of the waiting room. As we entered through the door I saw probably about four teens here in the waiting room. Well, that I knew. An estimated guess would say about ten altogether.

"Sam, Jesse," a girl hollered from my right. It was Mary. To her right was Dom. He gave a small weary wave. They both approached Jess and I. "Hey," Mary continued. "So glad you could come help —," she stopped. I saw she was watching Jess and nodded.

"Uh Mary, Dom, can I talk to you in the hall for a second?" Jess asked.

"Yeah," they said in unison. They walked in the hall waiting for Jess to follow.

"Alex," Jess called. He looked at Alex walking over. He leaned to his ear and whispered something. Alex nodded as Jess let go of my hand, kissed my cheek, and walked in the hallway. "What was that about?" I interrogated him. I squinted at Alex.

"Oh, that?" Alex said poking a thumb in the direction Jess, Mary, and Dom had disappeared to. I nodded and crossed my arms. Not in a mean way like I was trying to frighten him into telling me. It was just really creepy in here. After Jess and Alex's stories, I'm not a huge fan of hospitals. Especially this one. This is where Jess was over ten years ago. I forced myself to snap back to Alex.

"He just told me to make sure you were okay. That's all," Alex assured. He shrugged his shoulders. I wasn't so sure he was being completely honest with me. Actually I felt that no one, not even Jess, was being completely honest. What was with the major secrecy?

"Hey Sam," a really familiar voice said. The hair on my arms stood up as I looked in the direction of the voice and almost choked. I couldn't believe I recognized her by her voice. I've only ever heard her laugh. Never talking. Always laughing with five other people. Always laughing. At me. I motioned for Alex to walk away. I didn't want him to see what might happen. "Before you say you hate me or anything like that, I'm so sorry. I shouldn't have laughed when Crystal called you those awful names. I'm so sorry. You have every single right in the world to hate me. I know you can't forgive me for what I've done. I don't expect you to be my bestie or whatever. But all I ask is that you don't hate me." I saw tears fall from the girl's eyes. She put her head down and intertwined her hands.

I watched her. How every tear that fell had a drop of mascaraed pain. She had blonde ringlet curls, and had on a beautiful bright turquoise dress with matching wedges. Her glasses were big framed and magnified each tear. I took a step closer and put a hand on her shoulder. Just as I was about to speak up to her, I heard a word. It was a boy's voice. It was far too familiar. The one word just had to be a heartbreaking one. I turned in the direction bracing myself. I saw an all too familiar boy approach me. He told the girl he needed to talk to me alone. I took a step back, getting far too uncomfortable without Jess. The boy backed me into a corner.

"Well, well, well, Nigger. Come to see the damage people like you cause?" I could hear him sneer as he spoke his words. His eyes were icy blue that gave me a chill and were staring daggers at me. His dirty blonde hair seemed to be standing straight up with anger. All for me. But what had I done?

"Um, I-" I started.

The boy interrupted me and moved right into my face. He towered over me and I started to shake as my back hit the wall. "Yeah, excuse you. Excuse you from humanity because you're nothing, but a piece of shit! You're a bitch!" He slapped me. My head snapped to the right and I gasped, holding my cheek as tears streamed down my face.

Alex put a hand on his arm trying to pull him back. Nate turned and shoved him. Alex hit the floor with a thud and I heard his breath leave his lungs. "Stay out of this, fag."

"Stop!" I yelled. My face was throbbing.

Nate turned to face me. "You should just go back where you came from. You don't deserve a breath of air in your lungs. What you do deserve is to die in a hole. You and every single nigger left in this world! It's your kind's fault she's here!" he spat at me.

My heart stopped. Oh my gosh! What-

"And I'm not finished, so get the fuck out of here. You're not wanted and you're not fucking needed. That little change you wanna make, no one cares. Trash can't make a difference. So-"

"That's enough!" a raged voice said behind the boy. That voice. *Thank God.* I looked up to see a very furious Jess towering over the boy. I started to shake trying to stay in the present.

"You wanna say that again, Nate? I dare you to say that bull shit in front of me. Let's hear it." Jess's eyes were full of anger and aggravation. He stood tall and crossed his arms. Nate just looked up at Jess. He hid his fear in his eyes and just scoffed, crossing his arms to match Jess.

"Oh really. Nothing?" Jess continued. "Cause it just so happens, you're standing right in front of a hospital camera as well as a cell phone." He watched Nate look up at the camera and over to a phone recording everything. His fear was a little easier to see now. "You're lucky I don't beat your ass now." Jess paused and looked at the door of the waiting room opening. A police officer stepped inside. He turned to us and walked forward. I heard the clank of his handcuffs against his thigh as he walked. The tick tick of his shoes as they hit the polished floor. He stopped right next to Jess and Nate. He looked at Nate. He shook his head. "Hope it was worth it. You have the right to remain silent. Anything you say can and will be used against you in a court of law. You have the right to an attorney. If you cannot afford an attorney, one will be appointed for you," the police officer put him in cuffs as he read the rest of his Miranda Rights, leading him from the doors.

I felt myself sliding down the wall. A despicable pain ripped through me as I hit the ground. My tears continued to fall. I could barely see people walking up to me and leaning down. People asked me questions I couldn't understand. I saw a main face in front of all the others. I think it was Jess. I wasn't sure. I couldn't focus. I couldn't hear. Couldn't see. My heart hurt so much that the pain overwhelmed me. I was getting dizzy. I drifted into reality as hands grabbed both sides of my face. They were gentle and soft. I tried to bring my hands to rest on them, but couldn't move.

I heard muffled voices calling my name. Like people were speaking into a pillow. I couldn't focus. Couldn't think. I was in my mental bubble full of people who hated me because of my skin color. Hated me because they didn't know me. Because they were so ignorant in their own ways. My heart ached and I wanted to just die. I felt myself being pulled onto someone's lap and into their arms. It was getting harder and harder to hold back the black. I shut my eyes tightly and repeated Jesus, Jesus, Jesus.

All of a sudden, I felt an overwhelming feeling take over my entire body. There was a voice running through my head, except it wasn't mine. It was a strong voice. It said, "You are who I created you to be. You follow the path I have set out for you. You will accomplish great things, but people will always judge. But who are they to judge? I will look at their hearts. Have peace in knowing I know yours," then the voice left and was replaced by another voice.

This hushed voice said, "Sammi. Sammi! Please answer me. His opinion doesn't matter. You're you and you're beautiful for it. Please answer me, Sammi."

I opened my eyes and was able to see again. Able to move. I was in control of my own body again. I looked up at Jess who was watching me closely.

When he saw my eyes open, he pulled me closer to him in a bear hug. "Sammi, are you okay?" he asked worriedly.

"Yeah," I coughed, feeling my throat become extremely parched. "I'm, I'm okay. Just a little shhh... shaken up. That's all." I was surprised to hear my own voice. It was calmer than I would have ever imagined. A little shaky but that was it. I felt kinda cold and was shivering. I examined my surroundings as Jess continued to hold me. I saw Mary, Dom, Alex, and the other girl from the group all watching me with emotional faces. I still felt tears sliding, but did feel an odd ease, trying to ignore the embarrassment I felt. I pulled away from Jess and kissed his cheek. "Thank you for making that stop," I said truthfully.

"Of course. How could I let someone treat you like that?" he expressed as he pecked my forehead. His face stiffened as he placed his fingers by my eye. I winced a bit and he pulled back. He gave me a look letting me know he hadn't known everything that happened.

I nodded slightly and tried to change the subject. "And what's your name?" I asked, turning to the girl from before. She looked like she was hurt just as bad as I was.

"I'm Nicole and I can't believe Brad just did that. I'm so sorry. He's emotional right now. I hope you know you never did anything to deserve that. I'm so sorry. I hope one day you can find it in your heart to forgive me for being so stupid." She looked at the left side of my face and tears flooded her eyes again.

I put my hand on her shoulder. *Hopefully no one else has anything to say to me so I can finish this conversation.* "Of course I can forgive you. I can't hate you because you want to survive in a world where that type of stuff is cool unless you wanna be next." I stopped feeling a little light headed. I waited for the wave of nausea and throbbing to pass. She looked at me like I was absolutely, one-hundred-percent, crazy. So I continued. "Even though I may look a wreck, I'm okay. Even though what he said and... did..." I choked out, "hurt me so much, I can't hate him. I'm not made that way."

I watched her expression. She looked bewildered. She threw her arms around me. "I can't believe you could forgive me for all of those years of letting Crystal talk to you that way. Of just going along with it. You're amazing!" Nichole expressed.

I just threw an arm over her upper back, still feeling dizzy and the hurt still inside. I whispered, "I'm just me, but my God is pretty great."

Chapter 15

"Sammi, are you sure you're okay? You didn't speak to me for a while." Jess said as we sat down in some hospital chairs. They were green, plush, and for an odd reason, smelled of plastic. "Did you black out?" he asked, worried, lowering his voice.

I thought it was just a few seconds. "Yeah I'm okay. And I did, but Jess? God spoke to me... When I fell. I started," I cleared my throat, "going back, then heard this voice. It said stuff like 'you are who I created you to be,'" I informed Jess.

I felt him slide his arm over my shoulders. I leaned my head on his. "See Sammi? God is telling you to forget what they say. He's showing through you that it is possible to not hate someone who's treated you like that. You don't hate Nate. I have to work on that cause I hate him right now. If it wasn't for that camera and the video," he nodded up at the camera, "I don't know what I would have done." He shook his head, obviously disappointed in himself. "And he's lucky I didn't know he..." he trailed off and took his arm from around me. He put his elbows on his knees and ran his hands over his face and up through his hair. He clasped them together and looked down to the floor.

I rubbed his back. "I really do appreciate you making it stop."

"You shouldn't have had to take any of it. You don't deserve to be treated like that," he admitted. "But I wanted to hurt him. I can't believe he did that to you."

"Jess, you just wanted to protect me." I kissed his cheek and thanked him. He wrapped his arms back around me and we sat snuggled up in silence.

A nurse came through the doors followed by two adults with tears in their eyes. The nurse whispered a few things to them. They both nodded silently and left the waiting room. They were separated and kept a distance. The nurse turned her attention to all of us. "Are you all here for Miss Hanes?" Everyone nodded. "Okay, but only two people can go at a time. Your decision." She paused and waited for us to figure out who was going first.

"Uh, I think Sam and Jesse should go first," Dom recommended.

"Yeah, so do I," Mary and Nichole added.

Jess stood and grabbed my hand for me to stand up too. I did and we approached the
nurse. She nodded. "Okay. Follow me." We followed her through the doors through a thin, long, dull, white hall. There were closed doors on each side of the hall. We passed twenty-two rooms in a straight path before the nurse stopped outside of a closed door. "Now I warn you. She may not remember you. But just talk to her and see if you can't get her to remember anything. Okay?" she asked.

"We will," Jess replied. The nurse motioned for us to go in. I still had no clue who might be in this room. As we warily opened the door the nurse walked away. A curtain was blocking our view of the bed. I immediately smelled the disinfectants and the horrific stench of fresh blood. I shook it off and focused on the bed. Avoiding the masks and tools on the table.

We walked into the room and walked to the other side of the curtain. As soon as I saw the face I took a deep breath. I'm not too sure when I figured out it was her. Aside from the smile, she was an unbelievable sight. A part of her head was shaved. Taking the hair's place were a ton of stitches. The hair that was left was cut short and pulled to the side in a low ponytail. Her left eye was black and blue. And she had red cuts and yellow bruises all over her face. She had a splint on her nose and stitches in her left cheek, holding together a huge gash. She had a brace on her neck and a pink cast on her left arm. It had some signatures on it. On her left leg was another matching pink cast.

"Hey, I know you. You're that really nice girl from school, right?" Crystal asked.

I swallowed the knot in my throat and nodded slowly. "I'm Sam Adams." I didn't know what else to say. I saw Jess, in my side vision, step back.

"Sam Adams. I was once very mean to a girl named Sammi Adams. I wish I could apologize to her. She was best friends with that cute guy Jesse, then they started being a couple," she sighed. I turned my head in Jess's direction to watch him flash a confident smile. "And she was always so happy and never let anything in life get to her." I watched as Crystal poured her heart out to me, about me. Did she really not remember who I was?

"Really, Crystal?" I asked, astonished. "You don't know who I really am, do you?" I had to get her to remember me. Before she says something I'm not supposed to know.

"Yeah. You're Sam Addams. From school," she replied, looking at me like I was insane. Not knowing what to do, I just started to hum lightly. All she said was, "You have a really nice voice."

I motioned for Jess to come over and watched her eyes light up as he walked over so she could see him. "Jesse? Jesse Jackson?" she stumbled.

"Yeah, it's me." He grabbed my hand and kissed my cheek. I watched Crystal stare from
me, to Jess, then back to me.

"I'm Sammi, Crystal. It's me." I gave a small wave and braced myself just in case she
changed her mind on how she felt.

"Sammi? Is that really you?" she asked oddly.

"Yeah," I squeaked.

"I'm sorry..." she froze.

"It's okay," I said sitting by her legs.

"No it's not. I'm sorry. For me, for Nate... I can't believe that. They came in, asked me if I knew him, and said he'd been arrested." Her eyes dropped and I saw a tear run from her right eye.

I hesitated, then reached forward and gently wiped it away. "It's fine. Don't worry about the past. Worry about now. Focus on getting better." I gave a gentle smile.

"He... he didn't do that did he?" She looked at my face. I nodded slightly. "I'm sorry," she whispered again. "I didn't know he could do something like that..." she trailed off again. "He was so upset when I got hit. I'm sorry."

"It's not your fault," I assured her.

"But it is. But how can I be with someone like that?"

"Crystal, I know this is all a lot to take in, but focus on you right now. Get rest. Heal. Get better."

I watched her face relax slightly and she laid her head back against her pillow. She sighed. "I don't get it. How could you be so kind and forgiving after the horrible way I treated you?" she questioned me.

"The truth is, when you said those things to me that day, I was really hurt. I wanted to hate you. I can't lie. But God says to love each other. How can I do that if I hold a grudge against you? And I do forgive you, for everything." I gave her a reassuring grin.

She returned it. "So our slate is wiped clean?" she asked. I could see her eyes gloss over again.

"Of course. And I hope you know I didn't wish this upon you. I didn't wish you any harm," I informed.

"I know you didn't. It was my fault. We've always been told not to text and drive, but I didn't listen. I never thought I'd be the one. Look at the price I've paid for that thinking." She made a movement with her head that I think was supposed to be a shake.

"Sammi, come here?" Jess whisper-asked. I stood from the bed and came close. He whispered, "She's been talking about a lot that everyone said she wouldn't remember."

My eyes snapped open. "Omg..." I turned to Crystal. "Hey, Crystal? You remember the accident? And that Nate's your boyfriend? And our past?"

Crystal looked at me strangely. "Yeah. I remember. How could I not?" She watched me closely.

"Crystal, I was wondering if I could ask you a few questions."

"Shoot," she said, encouraging me.

"Who are your parents?" I began.

"James Williams and Lillian Hanes," she answered. "And where do you live?" I asked.

"Two-eleven on thirteenth street with my mom," she replied plainly. "How old are you?" I continued.

"Seventeen."

"Where do you go to school and what grade are you in?"

"Shaeffer High School. Gonna be a senior."

"So you do remember," I whispered. "I'll be right back," I said to Jess and whispered, "Ask her more questions. Keep her thinking. I'm going to get a nurse. I'll be back."

With that I exited the room and walked into the hall. I looked to the left, then to the right and found a nurse right away. "Excuse me ma'am! My friend Crystal remembers everything I've asked her or told her about." I filled in the nurse quickly on the questions I asked Crystal and told her the answers she gave me. As I finished, she followed me into the room. Jess was asking her what teachers she had in ninth grade.

"Excuse me, Ms. Hanes. The doctor is going to want to see you now that you have your memory back. I'll contact your parents immediately. You're going to be alright.." The nurse's words were true. She had a smile on her face. "I need you two to follow me so the doctor may speak to her and her parents." She flashed a smile.

As we followed her out the door, she shut the hospital room door and turned to us. "I don't know what you two did in there, but they will be grateful." She gave us one more smile and turned on her heel as we trailed behind her.

Chapter 16

"Good morning, Sammi! Happy Birthday!" Jess called as he entered my home. I smiled and threw my arms around his neck. I giggled, as always, as my feet left the ground.

"Hey, Jess. Thank you! Did you remember to take your allergy medicine this morning?" I asked.

"That I did," he ensured. "So," he continued as we sat down on the stools at my counter. "How are you holding up?" he asked. He took my hands in his and faced my palms out.

I felt my eyes squint somewhere off to the opposite side of the counter. It was weird. Nothing seemed to bother me about the last few weeks. All that came to mind from a first thought is the good things that occurred. Like us helping Alex, going to the adoption center and helping Brent, the lady asking us to start volunteering, my aunt and uncle adopting Alex, making amends with Nichole, and Crystal retrieving her memory. It wasn't until I pondered on it that I remembered the bad happening. "Hello! Earth to Sammi! You okay?" Jess asked, pulling my hand into his. I snapped back.

"Yeah. I'm okay." I took a deep breath to clear my head. "I'm just so ready to spend my day with you." I smiled.

"Awwww," Jess said, pulling me into a hug. I placed a small kiss on his cheek as he said, "That's my dream day." He laughed and kissed my head. "So what are we gonna do today for your birthday?"

"It'll just be me and you. Alex is hanging with my aunt and uncle. They took the day off to spend time with him. We are all coming back here once my mom gets off." I paused and looked out the window at the grey sky. The rain was falling so hard, I could hear the tick, tick, tick, tick of the rooftop.

"Would you be up for walking to my house?" Jesse asked. He got up and picked up his umbrella next to my door.

"I'm okay with that." I looked at the blue bordered clock that sits on the wall of the kitchen. It was ten forty-three.

I walked over to meet him, sliding on my tennis shoes as I reached him.

Jess grabbed his jacket and opened the door for me. I smiled, locked the handle on the door and stepped out under the hard downfall. I heard a drum roll as I stood under my roof. I watched Jess step out, shut the door, and open the umbrella. We stepped out from underneath the sheltered porch as he took my hand. We headed in the direction of Jess's house, and passed the place where the man had crawled out of his tent. Passed the clean park.

As I gazed out from under the umbrella, I looked down at the ground beneath my feet. I looked at the green plants that were squirming their way from under the concrete.

A small chill reiterated up my spine to the back of my skull and back down to the soles of my feet. I felt Jess let go of my hand and set his jacket on my shoulders, only to grab my hand again. "Thank you, Jess. I'm usually never cold walking in the rain." I looked up at him, smiled, then returned my eyes to the cement beneath my shoes.

"You're welcome, beautiful. Don't want you sick on your birthday." He gave a slight chuckle and a small warming smile. We ascended the steps to his house, putting the umbrella beside the door once we were safe under the roof. He opened the door, took a step forward and stopped. Before he led me in, he flipped his hood over my head which covered my face. He grabbed ahold of both of my hands and led me inside before I was able to take the hood from over my eyes.

"Happy birthday, Sammi!" I jumped as I heard multiple people holler the phrase. Then Jess's hood was pulled off my head as I caught sight of what was in front of me. An enormous happy birthday banner hung against the wall of Jess's kitchen. There were streamers hanging from the ceiling. A cake and presents on the table. I saw Alex, my mom, my aunt, my uncle, Mary, Dom, Nichole, Abby, Sarah, Alejandro, and a few other friends from school.

"Thank you," I returned. I went around in a circle hugging everyone, starting with my mom and ending with Jess. "You really didn't have to do all this Jess," I whispered to him.

"Yes I did. Remember my big birthday extravaganza?" He reminded me. "It was only fair."

"So Sam, how's it feel to be seventeen?" Sarah asked me. I looked up at Jess's tall, thin cousin, with beautiful mocha curls.

"It's exciting," I admitted, shaking off the sudden self hating thoughts.

"Good. It should be. Especially the presents part," she whispered to me.

"Oh, I see." I giggled as she winked and went to talk to my mom.

"Okay everybody," Mrs. Isabella called. "I, for one, am excited for Sam to see what I got her. So let's let her sit down and she can open them."

I watched as everyone took seats and took our cameras, ready to capture the important family moments. Jess led me to my "birthday seat". I sat down as Mr. Frank handed me the first present.

It was a big, wrapped box. I looked at the card taped to the gift. It was from Dom and Mary. I opened the envelope of the card and looked at the front. It was a colorful birthday cake. I read it aloud. It said

This cake looks like your personality.

I opened it up and it said

Colorful and fun! Promise to save us a piece!

Then I read the special messages silently and closed the card. I thanked Dom and Mary as I moved to the present. I tore off the wrapping paper and set it in the bag next to me. I looked at what sat on the table in front of me. It was still wrapped. So I began a process of unwrapping one layer of wrapping paper, to two layers, to seven. Then I finally got to a box. After unraveling about six more layers of wrapping paper I finally got to two DVD's. It was the extended editions of my two favorite movies. I gasped and looked to Dom and Mary. "Thank you guys so much! These are my favorites!"

"We heard!" they said in unison, smiling.

"Next," Mr. Frank called. I set my DVDs off to the side and got ready for the next one. This was a small bag. There was no card, but the little card attachment to the string said it was from Mrs. Isabella and Mr. Frank. I pulled out the bright orange tissue paper from the small bag and pulled out the contents inside. I took out three clear wrapped CDs and looked at the cover of each. All three were of my favorite bands.

I squealed with joy in my mind as I just simply flashed a huge smile. "Thank you, thank you, thank you!" I eventually squeaked. I hopped up and gave them both a huge hug.

They both smiled and returned it, slightly chuckling to themselves. "You are so welcome, Sammi. We know you love your CDs," they both expressed.

"Next," Mr. Frank called as I sat down. He handed me another box. This was a smaller box. I looked at the name on the card attached to the front. It was from my dad. I looked at my mom who smiled.

She said, "Before your dad died, he bought that for you. The last time we saw him in the hospital, he filled that card out just in case. He told me to save it for you," she summarized.

For a moment, I just stared at it. I looked at the wrapping paper that was my favorite color. It was a beautiful mixture of teal and turquoise. It had a big green bow that had the individual, curled ribbon running down in opposite directions. The box was about the size of a grown man's clenched fist. I slowly tore off the wrapping paper, watching the box with all of my attention as I set the ripped wrapping paper in the bag. I ran my finger around the plain black box. I cautiously opened it up and peered down inside. A folded up note was written in a style that could only be my father's handwriting. Tears welled up in my eyes as I unfolded it and began to read the note. It said:

My dear baby girl,

I am so so so sorry I had to leave you, my baby girl. God blessed me with you and your breath-taking mother. I know you probably miss me even though a great time has passed since our last meeting. I miss you too, my sweet little blessing. Always let God lead you and never turn away from Him. You are going to do wonderful things in this world, Samantha. You're going to be a strong and beautiful woman, which you are already becoming. I love you and always remember that! And when you have those nightmares, I will always be there to help fight them away. I'll see you again one day. Cancer can't keep me from you forever.
    I Love You My Little Miracle,
    Daddy

    By the time I had read the last word, I had a smile and tears streaming down my face. I felt strong comforting arms wrap around my waist from my left, a hand on my right shoulder and two on my left. I didn't even look, but immediately knew

Jess had his arms around me, my mom's hand was on my right shoulder, and Mrs. Isabella and Mr. Frank's hands were on my left. I remembered the box and looked down to see hidden under the note was a beautiful silver heart locket. In gorgeously scripted cursive is "The Heart Of A Beautiful Woman" in small neat letters. I pushed the small button on the side and the locket opened. On the left side was a picture of my mom, dad, and I. The other picture was of a young Jess and I holding hands, while sitting on a swing set. *I remember that day.*

    A few more tears fell as I was ripped away from my memories to feel another tear slide. I opened my eyes and smiled. I looked at all the faces surrounding me on my birthday. I stopped to meet Jess's eyes, my mom's eyes, Mrs. Isabella's, and Mr. Frank's eyes. I stopped at Mr. Frank and stood up. Never being quite skilled at putting on necklaces from behind, I thought I would need some help especially since I'm still shaky from the happy sobs. I looked at him with tears still in my eyes and asked, "Mr. Frank, would you be willing to help me with this?"

Mr. Frank nodded and took the necklace from the box and put it around me. *I respect and admire Mr. Frank. He is a true man of God.*

When he hooked it, I spun around and hugged him. "Thank you, Mr. Frank!" I muttered into his shoulder. The group around us stayed silent. I must have been quite a scene. When I released Mr. Frank, I walked in a huge circle to everyone who had shown up for me and I hugged each and everyone of them. My hug lingered a bit longer when I hugged my mom. I whispered a thank you and kissed her cheek. Then I hugged Jess and he kissed my forehead as I sat back down in my seat.

Then I heard the sweet coo of my mother's voice saying, "Alright, Sam. You have many more presents to open."

I adjusted my locket as I was handed another present. I could already tell this would be the best birthday of my life.

Chapter 17

"Okay, Sam. Two gifts left," Mrs. Isabella informed me. I looked at the box that sat in front of me. I slowly undid the turquoise wrapping paper to reveal a cardboard box. I opened it and pulled out a styrofoam outline and took that off as well. I felt my eyes bulge and my mouth drop. I looked at the beautifully sculpted glass that sat before me. The glass sculpture from the mall presented itself. I saw the brilliant light shine through and ran my eyes over the figures and scripture that made this sculpture what it was. I was snapped back to reality as someone slid a card under my hand. I had no idea who put it there, but quickly opened it to see who the card was from. The front of the card said:

    To A Girl Who Knows No
    Impossibilities,

The inside read:
    You know no impossibilities.
    You help others with their needs.
    You're thoughtful and kind.
    You have a beautiful mind

Full of ideas to better Humanity!
Happy Birthday to a true woman of God!
Love, Jess

And on the inside of the cover, I read his own personal note that stated

May God bless you on your very special birthday. I know God blessed me on this day seventeen years ago. I saw you looking at the glass sculpture in the mall and recognized it was your favorite scripture. So happy birthday and continue to let God move through you. Stay beautifully spirited, Sammi! <3

Immediately, I threw the card down and moved to Jess for an enormous hug. "THANK YOU, THANK YOU! YOU ARE THE BEST!" I screeched.

"Of course, Sammi! When we were at the mall and Alex was trying on his clothes, I went and waited outside of the store for you. I watched you stop at the sculpture stand. I saw that you really liked this one." He shrugged his shoulders like it was no big deal, when in fact it was a huge deal! He kissed my lips softly and held me for a few moments.

Jess and I pulled away from each other, blushing, when we heard a group 'Awwww'. I waited for the heat to fade from my cheeks and sat back down.

"Okay, last one," my mom replied.

There was a small gift bag that was placed in front of me. It was turquoise and had a gorgeous purple bow. Inside, there were two tickets inside for the upcoming Christian Jam Sesh concert! I was so ecstatic and looked frantically for who it's from. There was a small card attached to the string of the bag. All it said was "C".

Chapter 18

I look around. I'm in a dark room. There's people with tears in their eyes. There's a picture of a dear friend standing tall at the front of the room. Ian Harold. I see his mom and sister crying. A large coffin, closed, concealing its treasure inside. Everyone's dressed in their best black clothing out of respect for Al and his family.

I look to my right and see Jess. On my left, my mom sits watching. I wanted to cry, but I refused to and held strong as everyone quieted down. Alex's 13-year-old sister took the stand. "Hello. I'm Leah Harold. I've got a poem to share." And she began. "'Fighting the Battle' by Leah Harold.

The pain is here.
I feel it'll never leave.
Someone, close, fighting life means you fight it too.
My brother's letter declared war.
His last signature etched upon it.

He gives me a reason to fight.

The horrible sadness welling up inside, impossible to bear.

I can't lose the battle.

My family sobs and I think

"He lost the battle, but did he really?"

I will fight the battle of my brother's fleeting memory.

I'll see him in Heaven some day.'"

"No you won't!" A loud voice said. "He killed himself." We all looked around trying to find the person responsible for causing more pain on an already griefful day.

"You won't see him if you go to Heaven," another voice chimed in. "If there is a Heaven, he'll be going to the opposite of Heaven."

"Hell," another voice added.

"Stop it," I yelled and stood up. I was all too familiar with that accusation. "You don't know where he's at! You don't know what he said to God in his final moments." I spun looking for the person who would dare intrude a funeral.

I hear another voice say, "He didn't have enough faith in God!" What was going on? I couldn't find the people saying these things.

"If you can show me where in the Bible it says suicide takes you to Hell, I'll believe you." I cried as I kept spinning to find the voice.

"Even if he did believe in God. There are just some things that can't be forgiven. Killing yourself is only one." I got light headed and the room began to spin.

Another voice yelled through the fog filling the air. "Suicide is hell bound. Don't think you've escaped your damnation, Sammi. You're guilty, too."

I flew up and my eyes began to adjust to my room. I took a couple of deep breaths and collapsed with a sigh of relief. I looked over at my clock. It's 7:24. I prayed silently, thanking God for waking me and for peace that I needed and was sure he'd deliver.

I sat back up and swung my legs off the bed. I stood up and walked out of my room. I passed my mom's room, her door slightly ajar. I saw the time on her clock. 7:26. She'd be getting up for work soon. I walked down the steps and into the kitchen, turning on the lights. Then I pulled out eggs from the fridge, sausage from the freezer, and two pans from the bottom cabinets near my fridge. I turned on the stove, sprayed the pan, and sat it on the hot plate, just as I heard my mom's alarm go off. I heard the beeping stop and the creaking of floorboards.

    I turned my attention to the stove and put the sausage on and cracked the eggs in the pan. I grabbed a spatula and began moving the eggs around. I heard the bathroom door close. I looked at the time above the stove. 7:34. I dished the eggs and sausage on a plate and sat them at the table.

    I waited as the nightmare replayed in my mind. Ian's funeral is coming up and I guess the devil's testing my peace. Still, I had to prepare myself for those types of opinions. It's been four days since we learned the news, two after my birthday. It still hurt like it was fresh news

I flipped the sausage, lost in thought, when my mom entered the kitchen. "Morning, sweetheart. My beautiful baby girl. How'd you sleep?" she asked.

I answered, "Alright." I set her plate on the table and got the juice from the fridge.

My mom took my arm gently and turned me to look at her. She laid a hand on my cheek. "Another nightmare?" she guessed.

I nodded as she kissed my forehead. "You wanna talk about it?"

I smiled and shook my head. "Maybe later." I put her glass on the table and filled it with juice.

She returned the smile and sat down. I sat across from her and we prayed together. Then we ate. "So today," my mom began, "I'll be working until about 6:30, and so will Mrs. Isabelle and Mr. Frank. Are you going to pick up flowers and a card for the funeral?" She stopped and looked into my eyes. I nodded, feeling a small burning at the back of my eyes. I fought it and smiled.

My mom studied me a moment longer before saying, "It'll just be you and Jesse for a little while. Alex is going to the court to get his last name changed, today." I smiled immediately, thinking Alex was going to officially be my cousin and a part of our family. He's grown so much since we met him in the park a little over a week ago. Spiritually and physically. He's found forgiveness, peace, and love.

I nodded. "Okay. Jess and I can handle it." I took a bite out of my sausage.

My mom nodded. "I knew you could. Well, I better get going. Thanks for breakfast, hun." She stood and moved to clear the dishes.

I looked at the clock and stopped her. "I'll get it. You go on."

She smiled, came to kiss my forehead, and then smoothed my hair. "I love you, honey. I'll see ya later." Then she walked to the door and turned. She blew me one more kiss and left.

I cleared the table and stuck everything in the dishwasher. I put some soap in and turned it on.

Through the rushing water, I heard the doorbell ring. I walked over to the door and looked out the peephole and saw a smiling Jess. I opened the door and held it for him to come in. He took off his shoes and greeted me with a hug and a peck on the cheek. When he set me down he looked at me and said, "You look beautiful."

I looked down at my basketball shorts and tank-top, then shook my head. "Not right now," I said imagining the dry tears, and the type of hairstyle you only see on petrified people in corny, horror movies.

He grabbed my hands in his and kissed my forehead. "Especially now." I felt my heart skip a beat. He was too sweet. "Did you have a nightmare?"

"How did you know?" I asked even though I was well aware he could read my mind.

"Your self-confidence always goes down after you've had one," he answered.

I sat myself down at my table and he followed. He grabbed my hand as I nodded. "Do you want to talk about it?" he asked.

I slowly nodded again. "It was about tonight. The funeral." I felt my voice shake so I took a breath to steady it. Jess watched closely. "Someone said he went to Hell because he killed himself." I felt a tear fall thinking of anyone in a place like that. I closed my eyes trying not to even think about the possibility of my friend in eternal agony. I began to shake.

I felt Jess' arms around me and I buried my face into his chest. I don't know when, but I began to cry, and once it began, I couldn't stop it. All the emotions I had been holding in since I found out about Ian came pouring out. Sadness, disbelief, shock, heartache, and the worst of all, guilt. Guilt that I hadn't realized my friend's deep depression. The lingering guilt that made me feel like I could've done something about it, even if I couldn't have. I pushed away those thoughts. I felt my body shudder as Jess' arms constricted tighter. I felt warmth and comfort. He kissed my head. Feeling my mind trying to pull me deeper, I put a wall up in my head to keep me present.

My cries slowed and eventually, they stopped completely. I glanced up at Jess to see him already watching me, his eyes were full of worry and pain. "I'm sorry, Jess," I said, wiping my cheeks.

"For what?" he asked. "Compassion? Love? For hope that everyone can one day make it to Heaven?" He smiled and placed his hand along the left side of my face. I leaned into it. "Don't feel bad for having a heart for others, Sammi. Not many have them," he assured me. He looked into my eyes. "God's given you a heart to care because this world needs more people like you. People who care about others. I know it's a burden sometimes, but God knew he wanted you to have this heart. I'm sorry Ian is gone and I just wish I could talk to him one last time. I want to be mad at God that he is gone. But this wasn't God. This was Satan's fault. God had so much more planned for Ian than this. But what I do know is he will understand why Ian wanted to come home so soon."

I smiled, feeling slightly better. Jess always knew what to say. He was right of course. I attacked him in a hug, looping my arms around his neck. He brought his around me. I kissed his cheek and added, "Thank you. I love you."

When we pulled away, he said, "I love you. You're welcome, Sammi." He smiled at me and I returned it.

"So," I began, "We have to get flowers and a card today." Jess nodded. "Then we're free until 2:30. I'll go get ready."

"Okay," he said. I left him sitting at the kitchen table and went to get dressed in some jeans and a t-shirt. Then I made my bed, fixed my hair, grabbed my necklace, and headed back downstairs.

When I met Jess, I asked, "Can you put this on for me?" He smiled and nodded. I felt the cool metal lay against my skin and looked down at the heart-locket. I thought of my dad and my birthday. I felt Jess clasp it shut, and then I turned to face him. "Thank you," I said.

He returned it. "You're welcome. Where are we going first?" he asked.

I shrugged. "Maybe the flower shop to get the order in?"

Jess nodded and moved to put his shoes on. I followed suit and then he held the door open for me, and I stepped out onto the porch. Jess locked the door and grabbed his umbrella, shutting the door behind him. He opened it and we walked out into the rain together. I wrapped my arms around Jess's arm that held the umbrella. He smiled down at me and I smiled back. I looked to see the rain hit off the pavement. Saw it running down the road and twirling into a drain. I heard the soothing pitter-patter all around us. Felt its calm, peaceful welcome.

Eventually, we made it to 'Tina's Flowers', a small shop two blocks down from my house. We walked in and Jess shut the umbrella. He left it by the door and we went to the lady at the counter. Her name-tag read 'Tina'. She was shorter with strawberry-blonde hair and a friendly smile. "Hello," Jess said with a pleasant smile. "We need a dozen lilies."

"Well you've come to the right place," Tina confirmed with a small smile. She wrote something down on a notepad and asked, "What time do you need 'em by?"

"2:30," Jess replied. He gave my hand a light squeeze.

"I've been gettin' lots of orders for that time. A funeral for a young man," she said and I felt a slight pain in my heart.

"Yeah, that's it," Jess replied. I smiled at Jess who was calm and collected in light of everything. He always managed to keep it together, to help keep me together.

"Okay. That'll be," she said, punching in a few numbers on a cash register, "Eight dollars. And I'll give you the message for free," she added.

"Thank you," I finally said. "We can pay, though," I assured.

"No, that's alright. That young man seemed to have had a lot who cared for him. There must've been somethin' really special there. I'd be glad to help give back somethin'." She smiled a light, condoling smile. "So, what'll the message be?" she asked, pen ready.

I thought for a moment and then said, "To our best friend we won't ever forget. Hopefully one day, we'll see you again." I didn't realize the words I'd said until they came out. I guess that was one of my biggest fears. That I wouldn't ever see Ian again. Either from his doing, or mine.

Chapter 19

"You picked a really nice card, Sammi," Jess told me as we walked out of the small shop in the mall.

"Thanks," I said as he reached for my hand. I squeezed it lightly. "You wanna get something to drink?" I asked. He nodded. We headed to the elevator and went up a few floors to the food court. I smiled.

"What are you thinking?" Jess asked me like he didn't already know.

Zoning out, I answered "I'm thinking about the man we met in here. About how you helped change his life." I saw Jess smile a bright smile.

"I think about him sometimes, too. I wonder how he's doing. If he ever really did call his family, or if he turned himself around." The elevator doors opened and we walked out. "What are you thirsty for?" Jess asked me as we walked up to "Freezies".

"Um..." I thought. "Strawberry and banana please." I pulled out my wallet and, as if on cue, Jess put his hand over it and shook his head.

"I'm paying," he assured, pulling out his wallet. I smiled knowing there was no way he wouldn't pay. I slid it back into my bag as Jess ordered and paid.

We got our drinks and sat down together at a two-person table that faced each other. I took a small sip of mine and looked up at the glass roof. I saw the rain hit and pour off of the sides.

I felt Jess lay his hand over mine. "Are you okay, Sammi?" he asked, watching me closely.

I knew he knew exactly how I felt, but he asked to see if I was ready to talk about it. "I'm okay, I just am kinda spacey. I'm thinking about a lot of different stuff," I admitted.

He rubbed my hand. "I could tell. I'm here if you want to talk, and I'm here if you don't."

I smiled and looked into his eyes. "Thank you," I said genuinely.

He chuckled. "There's no reason to be thankful. I care about you and will always be here for you." He smiled and gazed into my eyes.

"For that," I began, "I am thankful." I returned the smile.

Then a huge crack of thunder hit and I jumped a little. Jess rubbed my hand. "The

angels are bowling," he said.

I laughed lightly and took another sip of my drink. I felt my phone vibrate in my pocket

and pulled it out. It was Mary. I pushed answer. "Hi, Mary."

"Hey, Sammi. I'm with Dom right now. We were wondering what type of flowers we should get for later. We weren't sure." I heard the rhythmic pattern of rain sounding on the phone.

"Well, Jess and I got lilies. Those are Mrs. Harold's favorite. Leah's favorite are orchids. But I think any will be fine," I replied. I saw Jess watching me. I mouthed "flowers". He nodded.

"Okay, Sammi," Mary said. "Thank you!" she called.

"You're welcome. See ya later. Bye."

"Bye." I heard Dom say bye, too. Then we hung up.

"They wanted to know what flowers to bring for tonight?" Jess asked. I nodded. "It's crazy how much things have changed lately. You and I are in the news, we meet new friends, you gain a new cousin and more. All in a few weeks," he finished.

I nodded. It's too bad we had to lose someone special in the process. That wasn't God tho. But God's been so good to us. Helping us to take a stand and make a difference. Another year older. A growing family. "God's been good."

I hadn't noticed I'd said it aloud until Jess said, "He has."

"So," I said looking up at him. "What do you wanna do?" I asked.

Jess looked at the clock on the wall. 9 a.m. "Well, I've gotta get a black shirt. You wanna just walk around the mall?" he asked.

I nodded. "I need to get a black dress." Jess and I have only ever been to one funeral. That was back when my dad died. So we didn't exactly own the proper clothing.

"Sounds like a date," he replied, standing up. I followed suit, grabbing our bag and drinks, and took the elevator down one floor. We went into a store and Jess and I went back to the button-down shirts. He picked out a few and went to the changing room. I waited by the ties and looked for a nice black one. I found a solid one and held it in my hand. Jess came out and asked, "What do you think?"

I nodded and smiled. "That one's nice." I held up the tie and hung it around his neck. He smiled. "Perfect." He disappeared back into the changing room. He came out in a moment and we headed to the girls' side.

I saw a few nice black dresses. It felt odd buying such fancy clothes for a funeral. To dress so nice and for people to compliment each other felt so weird in such a setting. Fear swelled in my throat, worrying I'd get very used to this dress.

Chapter 20

I looked in the mirror. Black dress, black shoes, black hair-tie, black jacket, black purse. I heard a knock downstairs and headed down.

I looked through the peep-hole and saw Jess. I opened it and let him in. He had his black button-down shirt on, black pants, black tie, and black shoes. "You look nice," Jess said, taking off his shoes. I put all my stuff down at the table. Then we sat down.

"Thanks," I said, then added, "You, too." I smiled. He really did. I looked at the clock when I felt my phone vibrate. It read Crystal. I opened the text.

'Hey, Sammi. I was wondering how you were doing. I know Ian's funeral is today.'

I replied, 'Alright. How about you?'

Her text came quickly. 'I'm doing well. I can leave on Friday. Two days.'

I smiled knowing she was healing well from the car accident. 'That's great!' I answered. I sent it and looked over at Jess.

I updated that it was Crystal and she can leave the hospital Friday.

He nodded as I got the next one. 'Yeah, but how are you?'

I sighed. 'I'm okay, I guess. I'm sad, but I know God's got a plan for this.' I felt a tear come to my eye and run down my cheek. Jess wiped it.

'You're a strong girl, Sammi.'

I wrote, 'Says the one who's getting out of the hospital two months early.'

The reply was speedy. 'That's a different type of strength, Sammi.'

I began typing, feeling very self conscious. 'I wouldn't exactly call myself strong.' I replied. I honestly felt that way. Especially because as often as I wake up crying, am so insecure, and am very emotional. I just didn't really see "Strong Sammi". I knew I had God, but I also knew I wouldn't be able to do anything without him.

'I would.' she wrote back. I was going to reply, but I got another one. 'I know you're gonna write you aren't but you are. I never would have messed with you for so long if you weren't. Now, take care. I've gotta go for some X-rays. Talk to ya later.'

I replied 'Bye, Crystal.' Then closed my phone and slid it in my purse. Jess laid his hand on mine. "Are you okay?"

I nodded looking at the table. "I just wish I saw myself as others saw me. Crystal said I was strong. How am I strong?" I asked quietly. I think the last part was meant more for me than Jess.

Jess still answered. "You are asking how someone who lost their dad so young, who has been bullied all her life, who has nightmares of the past and scary futures all the time, and who cares so deeply for others, is strong?" He looked at me in disbelief. "That's your question?"

"That stuff makes me weak. Not strong." I closed my eyes as I felt them heat up. I didn't want to cry. Not as we were talking about being weak.

"Sammi, do you honestly think you're weak because you hate the evil in the world? Because your heart bleeds for others?" Jess took both of my hands in his and I looked into his eyes. "Do you honestly feel that way?"

As I looked into Jess' eyes, I didn't know what I thought. I didn't know how I felt, or why I felt it. I was hurting, but from what I didn't know. My self confidence was so low and I felt like I'd never be strong and confident. "I don't know how I feel anymore."

"Sammi, if you can believe no one else on this earth, believe me. You are strong. Though you can't see it, you are. Everything you've gone through has made you who you are now," he paused. "Remember back when I first told you about my parents and what they did?" I sniffled and nodded. He continued, "And I told you I'd never be okay? That I'd never feel safe?" Again, I nodded. He let go of one of my hands and pointed to himself. I knew exactly where he was going. "That same kid," he paused, "is right here. He never got replaced. He just found hope and peace. He got past the dark tunnel and into the sun." He grabbed my hand again and brought them both to his lips.

I smiled, feeling a little better, then frowned as a new thought came. "That's because you are strong, Jess. Look at all you've been through." I shivered thinking about it all. "I haven't been through half the crazy stuff you've been through, and I can't even handle small things."

"Sammi, do not compare your problems to anyone else's. Nothing you've been through has been small. They made you who you are. The kind, compassionate, loving, understanding, beautiful, Christian girl you are. And 'sensitive'?" he said, moving his fingers to make quotation marks. "That makes you more determined to help and love others. It's a gift, not a curse. You love others so much, Sammi, but give none to yourself. And, believe me, there's a lot to love about you," he insisted. "You've just got to look for it."

I wrapped my arms around Jess and held him tight. As Jess returned the hug, I knew he was right. God didn't make mistakes. Everything happens for a reason and everyone lives for one, too. I knew by criticizing myself, I was criticizing God's masterpiece. I knew that. It was just time to believe it.

....

"Thank you for coming," Ms. Harold said, hugging Jess and I tightly.

"We wouldn't have missed it. He was a great friend and a wonderful person," Jess said. I felt his hand in mine and held onto it tight. I wanted to cry, needed to, but I had to stay strong.

"Thank you," Ms. Harold smiled. We saw a tear fall. "You have no idea how much that means to me. Ian talked about you two often. He knew no matter what happened, he always had the two of you. He even wanted to know more about God because of you, two. I don't know if he ever would've been the God loving man he was without you two." I saw her smile bigger and sniffle. "Thank you for having a positive impact on my son, Sam and Jesse. You have no idea the peace you two have brought me."

I smiled and tried desperately to hold my tears in. "He made just as much of an impact on us. He loved you and Leah so much. We'll be praying for you," I said. Then I added, "Please, let us know if you need anything. Leah, too."

Ms. Harold pulled us in another hug. "Thank you."

When she let us go, we headed to see Leah. She smiled, sadly when she saw us. She gave me a big hug, and then hugged Jess. "You did such a wonderful job singing," I said.

She smiled. "Thanks." I saw tears come to her eyes. "Why did he have to go, Sammi? Why did God let him leave us?" I knelt down and pulled her into a tight hug as she began to cry. She looped her arms around my neck and held onto me so tight. I rubbed her back and smoothed her hair. I felt her tiny body tremble in my arms.

I stayed silent for a moment, thinking. Then I said, "I don't know what your brother was facing before he left. I don't know what the Devil was making him believe. But what I do know is God is a gentleman. He will never force himself on us. He gives us free will to make our own decisions. I do believe someone was using their free will to make Ian want to leave. God didn't want it. He had an amazing plan for Ian. But I knew his heart. I do believe we'll see him again. I know you'll miss him, but he isn't really gone. You've still got the memories with him. And he loved you more than I've ever seen someone love their sibling. He never wanted to miss a dance recital, a soccer game, a softball game, or even be late to pick you up, Leah. For Christmas and birthdays, he saved for months just to get you exactly what you wanted. Wherever he is now, that hasn't changed, hun."

I felt Leah pick her head up from my shoulder. She wiped her tears and smiled slightly. "Thank you, Sam. I love you." She sniffled and hugged me tight again.

"I love you, too, Leah," I replied. Then, we pulled apart and I kissed her forehead. "It'll get easier one day. Just always remember the time you did have with him."

"I will, Sam. Thank you." Then she moved to go talk to one of her grandparents. Jess grabbed my hand again and gave a small smile. We headed for the door and walked outside. We began the walk towards my house. "You were great with Leah, Sammi."

I thought back. "I just wanted to make her feel better. It wasn't anything out of the ordinary."

He squeezed my hand. "Nothing out of the ordinary for you, but definitely for most people. Sammi, you put your feelings aside, without even realizing, and help those who are in need. Most people are so selfish that they don't think about how anyone else feels."

I never really thought about it that way. It was just like with little Brent. Jess had said about the same thing then. "Thank you, Jess," I said. I really had to get a new perspective on myself. I thought back to our conversation with Ms. Harold. "Did you have any idea that we made that much of an impact on Ian?" I asked.

"Honestly, not at all, but it's a little confirmation that we're doing something right." We stopped, looked both ways and crossed the street.

I stayed silent for a moment and thought about what he said. He was right. We walked up onto my porch and I grabbed my key. "I'll be back in fifteen minutes. I'm going to change and feed the fish in the pond," Jess said. "Then we can go get something to eat."

I nodded and smiled. "Alright. I'll see you soon." He kissed my cheek and walked back down the stairs. He waited to make sure I got in okay, and then headed down the street.

I walked up to my room and changed out of my funeral clothes. I put on jeans and a tank top and went back downstairs to the living room. I turned on the TV, watched a movie, and waited for Jess.

Chapter 21

I looked up at the clock and saw it had been half an hour. I checked my phone and didn't see a text. I focused on the TV for another half an hour and then checked my phone again. When I saw I didn't have any messages, I called Jess. It went straight to voicemail. His phone was off.

I stood and gathered my things. I figured I'd just meet him over at his house. I tied my jacket around my waist, grabbed my purse, and headed out the door. I locked it behind me and began the walk to Jess'. Eventually I passed the park. I smiled. It still looked very clean.

Jess' house came into view and I heard screeching tires pull away. I began to run. Jess' door was wide open, and I got a really bad feeling in my gut. I sprinted to his door and ran inside. I looked around. The kitchen was a mess. Tables and chairs were flipped on their sides, and miscellaneous objects were scattered along the floor. I walked through the house carefully, and smelled alcohol and another smell I couldn't quite name. "Jess?" I called out. I stepped towards the back door, seeing it was open as well. I looked around and gasped. "Jesse!" I ran to him and knelt down beside him. I pulled my phone out and called the police.

"What is your emergency?"

"Someone's been hurt! Please, I need an ambulance! 259 King Boulevard. We are in the backyard. You have to come through the house. Please hurry!"

"We are dispatching vehicles to your location." I pulled the phone from my ear and looked down at Jess. He was wheezing and holding his stomach tightly. He had a black eye, and what looked like a broken nose. His hair was matted with blood, and he had cuts and bruises on his arms and legs. There was blood seeping through his shirt. I untied my jacket from my waist, and used it to put pressure on the spot he'd been holding.

"Sammi, I couldn't fight them," he seethed. He held his head tightly in his hands.

"Fight who, Jess?" I asked. I pushed hard and heard him wince, but I had to do it.

"My parents and uncle. They were here. I couldn't fight them." I froze for a moment. Jess's parents. The ones who almost killed him multiple times before he turned five? The parents who were supposed to be in jail for the rest of their lives?

I snapped out of it as I heard the sound of an ambulance. "Jess, the ambulance is almost here." I felt my heart shatter. This was worse than the dream I had before about Jess and our families. This was real and Jess was hurt severely. He never let me see him in pain. He never let anyone see him in pain, but I saw it then. I heard his rapid breathing and felt his chest shutter. Felt the hot, sticky blood on my hands from my jacket.

"Paramedics!" someone called.

"We are in the back. Hurry!" I called. I watched Jess struggle and my heart ached. "You're gonna be okay," I whispered. He locked his pain-stricken eyes on mine. "You're gonna be okay."

The paramedics came in with a board. They laid it beside Jess and I moved to the side. I watched them lift Jess onto the board and strap him in. They lifted it and moved towards the house again. I followed. As they loaded him into the ambulance, another paramedic asked me how old I was.

"Seventeen," I replied.

"You can ride with him, then," she said. I nodded and got into the ambulance. I sat next to Jess and gripped his right hand in my left one. He looked up at me with pain in his eyes. I felt tears prick mine, but I refused to cry. The paramedics began to cut Jess' shirt off to see what was causing the blood. There was a gash about five inches long near his collarbone, but a deep one down his abdomen about seven or eight inches long. His chest was green, black, purple, and blue.

The male paramedic radioed, "We have a teen in critical condition. He needs immediate medical service." We felt the ambulance lunge forward and the siren began to blare. The male medic put an IV in Jess' arm, while the female medic put a mask over his mouth and nose. It made a noise and the mask fogged up. The man took a comb softly through Jess' hair, and the woman began to bandage his chest. I felt like I was going to throw up, so I kept my eyes on Jess's. We felt the ambulance slow and come to a stop. The doors burst open and I kissed Jess's forehead. I watched them lift him out and wheel him to the entrance. I jumped out and followed suit until the nurse stopped me, and said I had to wait in the waiting room. Instead, I moved back outside. I pulled my phone out and called my mom.

"Hi, sweetie. What's up?"

"Mom! Jess got jumped by his parents and uncle! I called the police, and now we are at the hospital, and he's hurt bad!" I rambled out.

"What?! Oh my gosh. Isabella! Frank!" I heard her call. "Jess is at the hospital! We've got to go!" She spoke to me again. "Sammi, we will be there in twenty minutes."

"Okay." Then I hung up the phone. I felt my heart pounding and my breathing rapid. I paced for a while. Eventually, I couldn't fight off the tears anymore. I sat against the wall, tucked my head into my arms and began to cry.

....

"Excuse me, miss?" An officer said. "Are you Samantha?" I nodded. The man and his partner sat in the seats across from me in the waiting room. "Do you mind if we ask you a few questions about Jesse Jackson?" His name tag read 'Officer Reynolds'.

I shook my head. "I don't mind. If I can help in any way, I will."

"Can you tell us what happened?" the lady asked. Her badge read 'Officer Stewart'.

"I wasn't there. I have no idea. All I know is Jess said his parents and uncle did it to him,"
I replied.

"Is that what his friends know him as? Jess?" Officer Reynolds asked. He had a pen and paper.

I shook my head. "Everyone, but me, calls him Jesse."

Officer Reynolds nodded and scribbled. "Can you tell us what you did see? Were you
with Jesse before then?"

I nodded. "We had gone to Ian Harold's funeral. Then, we were on our way back to my house. He left to get changed and to feed his fish in his pond. He said he'd be back in fifteen minutes. An hour had passed and I figured that I'd meet him there. I left and-" I paused. It felt like there was a knot in my throat the size of a grapefruit. My eyes began to burn and I felt a tear fall. I wiped it. I forced myself to continue. "When I got there, a blue car sped away from Jess' house. I began to run. I noticed the front door had been left open. It smelled bad inside and the house was a mess. I ran out back." I stopped again and wiped my tear-streaked cheeks. "That's when I saw him," my voice squeaked.

"I'm sorry you had to see that, Samantha," Officer Stewart said.

"Did Jesse tell you anything else?" Officer Reynolds asked. I shook my head. "He just said he couldn't fight his parents.

His uncle was there, too. He kept saying he couldn't fight them."

Officer Reynolds stopped for a moment. "Do you have any idea why he couldn't fight
them? I've seen Jesse. He's a big guy and it seems he could have at least fought back to get away." He looked stunned. "Seems odd he wouldn't."

"When Jess was younger, his parents abused him often. They'd almost killed him quite a few times. His aunt and uncle saved him and his parents went to jail. Jess used to tell me that he never fought back. He was only five, but he wouldn't do anything but scream, unwillingly. He just never could touch his parents. He loved them, despite what they did. He couldn't and wouldn't raise a hand to his parents." I took a breath aware of the hollow aching in my heart. I continued. "I think it's the same for now. Despite everything, he still will not lay his hands on them. Also, his uncle and dad are both huge guys, and his mom isn't small either. She was a fighter in high school. If someone even looked at her wrong, she was fighting them. If they triple teamed him..." I stopped as I felt more tears fall. I wiped my cheeks and looked at my hands.

I felt a hand on my shoulder. I looked to see Officer Stewart had moved to sit next to me. "You did well, Sammi." I smiled. "And we know who you two are. You've done some impressive things recently. We'll be in touch." She smiled. I looked to see Officer Reynolds nod and smile, too.

"Thanks," I replied.

"Sammi!" my mom called, rushing into the doors. I leaped up and went to hug her. She wrapped her arms around me and whispered, "My baby. I'm so sorry."

"Excuse me, ma'am?" Officer Stewart asked.

"Hello, officer," my mom greeted me.

"I'd just like to say you have a wonderful girl here. You've raised her well. Jesse is very lucky to have her. Especially today," Officer Stewart said.

"Thank you. I know I do. And I know he is," my mom replied. She soothes my hair with her hand as her other one wrapped around me.

"Sam!" Mrs. Isabella called as she and Mr. Frank ran in. They rushed to me and hugged
me tight. When they let go, everyone gasped. They saw the dried blood on my shirt and hands. Mrs. Isabella began to cry. "Our baby!" Mr. Frank pulled her into him tightly. She cried into his chest. I wanted to cry again, too.

"I'm sorry to interrupt, but I think we can tell you guys what Samantha's said. I don't think she needs to repeat that again. If you'll follow me," Officer Reynolds said, opening a conference room door. My mom, Mrs. Isabella and Mr. Frank all filed in behind him.

As I sat down, the door opened and Officer Stewart came back out with a shirt. "Here. Would you like to change out of that shirt?" I looked down at my shirt and nodded. She gave it to me and I went to the bathroom. I changed out of the tank top and into the t-shirt that said "Philippians 4:13- I can do all things through he who gives me strength." Mrs. Isabella must have brought a change of clothes for Jess, but gave me the shirt.

Though it was huge on me, I took as much comfort in the verse as I could.

I came out of the bathroom and handed the shirt over to Officer Stewart. She slid it in a
bag. "We'll get this back to you."

I shook my head. "Keep it. I don't want it back." I didn't want anything reminding me of
this day. I went and sat back down in the waiting room. Then, I cried silently to myself for about the fiftieth time that day.

Chapter 22

"Jesse Jackson?" Mr. Frank, Mrs. Isabella, my mom, and I all stood. "He's gonna be fine." We all let out a deep breath. "He just got out of surgery. He'll need some time to heal, though. He has a minor concussion from blunt-force-trauma, multiple contusions, five broken ribs, and a sprained leg. But like I said," the doctor continued, "he will be okay and will go back to normal. It'll just take time."

"Can we see him?" Mrs. Isabella and Mr. Frank asked.

The doctor nodded. "But one at a time." He waited.

"Mr. Frank and Mrs. Isabella, should go first and second," I said.

"Are you sure, Sammi?" they asked.

"Yes," I assured them. "Go see him."

Mr. Frank let his wife go first, and the rest of us sat back down. My mom slid her arm
around me. "I'm so sorry, Sammi," Mr. Frank said for about the thirtieth time. "You shouldn't have had to see that."

"It's okay, Mr. Frank." I gave a reassuring smile. "I'm just worried about him."

"I know you are, baby," my mom said. "I'm sorry. Why don't you go in last and you can have some time to talk with him." She rubbed my shoulder. I nodded and she kissed my head. I yawned. I was utterly exhausted physically, mentally, and emotionally. So much sadness and fatigue welled up inside, I was afraid it was going to swallow me up whole. I pulled my knees up to my chest, and wrapped my arms around them. Wanting to try to relax, I laid my cheek on my knees, hoping to not think for a moment. I didn't wanna cry, and I didn't want to think about anything that happened. Didn't want to think about the past. For a second, I just needed to stop and breathe.

Eventually, Mrs. Isabella came out. She had tears in her eyes. Mr. Frank encased her in a hug, pulling her close. She pulled away and smiled sadly. "He's banged up, but he's okay. He's in there smiling and excited to see us all. Such a strong boy." Her sad smile grew.

Mr. Frank let her go and headed in after the doctor. Mrs. Isabella sat on the other side of me. She put her arm around me. "He's worried about you, Sammi."

"He shouldn't be," I began. "He's gotta focus on getting better." Jess shouldn't be worried about me.

"Jesse may be the one who got hurt, but you had to see it. He knows you're worried about him, Sammi. He knows that you walked in on him after. You had to call the ambulance and take care of him until they got there." Mrs. Isabella rubbed my shoulder. "He can't wait to see you, though." She smiled brightly.

That made me feel a little better. I wanted to see him, too. To get the image of Jess earlier out of my mind. To see him okay. I felt like I was gonna cry again, so I buried my face in my knees.

After about fifteen minutes, Mr. Frank came out into the waiting room with the doctor, and my mom stood. "I'm heading in, and then you'll be up, Sammi."

I nodded. "Okay."

Mr. Frank came and sat on my other side. "He is very excited to see you, Sammi."

I smiled. I wanted to see him. *But what will I see?*

Mr. Frank and Mrs. Isabella both gave me a hug from each side. "Thank you, Sam!" Mrs. Isabella said. She kissed my temple. I didn't really know why I deserved all the "thank you's". Mrs. Isabella added, "And not just for today. Thank you for always being there for him. Thank you for being his best friend. Thank you for being such a wonderful girl. We are all so lucky to have you in our lives, Sam."

That brought tears to my eyes. I sniffled and hugged Mrs. Isabella. I laid my head on her shoulder. She held me tight as Mr. Frank rubbed my back. I held back any more tears. I needed to be strong. These are Jess' parents. He is their son, even if not by birth. They shouldn't be comforting me.

When my mom came out, I stood slowly. She met me with a big hug. "He's so excited to see you, Sammi." She smiled and kissed my head. I nodded and followed the doctor.

I don't know about anyone else, but when I walked down the hall to the hospital room, it felt like the longest walk of my life. My hands were shaking and my heart was beating fast. I didn't know what I would see when I'd get to the room. My mind was racing. I took a deep breath to try to relax, and to keep my knees from buckling underneath me.

At the end of the hall we made a right and got to room 149. The doctor stopped and motioned for me to step in. I did and was met with, "Sammi!" Jess was smiling. He had a bandage around his head, a brace on his left leg, an IV in his left arm, and a hospital gown on. He was laying in a bed, his head slightly elevated. His black eye was still there, but the swelling had gone down.

I returned the smile and went to his side. I kissed his forehead. "Hey, Jess. How are you feeling?"

"Better. It's good to see you." He took my hand in his. His movements were slow and he winced every so often. "How are you?" he asked.

"I'm fine. You're the one who needs to get better," I answered.

"Yeah, but I know you, Sammi." He paused and took a breath. "I'm sorry you had to see that. I'm just happy you weren't there."

"I should have stayed with you, though," my voice cracked. I felt my inner wall almost break. My emotions were flooding over, and I was trying to keep them shut in. "I should have been there with you. Maybe they wouldn't have done what they did if someone was there with you."

"Sammi," Jess began. "There was nothing you could have done. I didn't want you there." His voice dropped to a whisper and he looked away. "They would have hurt you, too."

I knew he was right, but I couldn't help but wonder if it would have turned out differently had I been there. "Why didn't you fight back, Jess?" I asked. My voice cracked again.

"I hesitated. They were my parents. Then, it was too late anyway. My uncle and dad grabbed me. I couldn't fight back. But if you were there," he paused and looked up at me. "There wouldn't have been any hesitation."

I felt tears come to my eyes. "Jess." I didn't want to cry, but tears ran down my cheeks. I wrapped my arms around his neck and he wrapped his arm around my waist. He held me close, but I was so careful. I didn't want to break him. He rubbed my back as I cried. "I'm so sorry."

"Don't be. You didn't do this," he said in a soothing voice. He held me close until my sobs ceased. When they did, I lifted my head up and saw him smile. "You didn't do this. You have no reason to be sorry. I wish you hadn't seen anything, but thank you for finding me." He kissed my lips gently. I melted momentarily, just so happy to be with him. To see him and feel his heart beating. To know he was okay.

I pulled away from him and slid a chair over. I sat down next to him and slid my left hand in his right one. He squeezed it reassuringly. "I'm glad, too." Even though I wished I hadn't seen it, I'm still glad I did. If I didn't, he could have been there, alone, for a very long time. I didn't want to think about that possibility.

"Did they have a knife?" I heard myself ask. I guess my subconscious just needed to know what happened, despite being deathly afraid to hear the answers.

"It doesn't matter," he said. I knew he was trying to protect me.

I gave him a look. "Jess, I need to know what happened to you."

He stayed silent for a while. Then, he slowly consented with a deep exhale. "Yeah, they did. Two."

"What else?" I asked.

Jess gave me a questioning glance. "Who said there was more?"

"The doctor said that you had blunt-force-trauma," I stated matter-of-factly.

He let out a deep breath. "My mom had a bat." He looked up at the ceiling.

"Please don't call her that. She may be your birth mother, but she is not your mom, Jess. Your mom is out in the waiting room with your dad, scared out of their minds. Those are the people who love you," I reminded him.

He smiled up at me. "I know." He went to adjust himself in the bed and I heard him seethe. He almost kept a straight face, but he couldn't hide it from me.

"Did they give you anything for the pain?" I asked.

He nodded. "They just can't give me too much because of the drowsiness. I'm not supposed to go to sleep for a while." I nodded. "Have you heard from Alex? Did everything go okay?" he asked, changing the subject.

I shook my head. "I turned my phone off after I called my mom. I didn't want to talk to anyone." I slid my phone out of my pocket, and turned it on. When it came on, my phone went crazy with all of the texts I'd missed. I had four from Crystal, one from Mary, six from Alex, three from Sarah, and one from the lady at the Adoption Agency.

"Go ahead and answer them," Jess said. "I've got time." He smiled. I kissed his cheek.

I scrolled through Crystal's with one hand, keeping the other one in Jess's. They were just asking me how I was from the funeral, if I needed anything that she'd be there, and stuff like that. Mary's was just that she tried to catch me at the funeral, but she must have missed me. Sarah's were all asking about Jess, and the group home was wondering if we were free to come next Wednesday. I replied a quick text to Crystal and Mary, like 'Sorry. I've been super busy. I'll text you when I get a chance.' To the agency I said, 'I'd have to check. Thanks. I'll get back to you.' I didn't think Jess would be better in a week. To Sarah, I wrote, 'He's alright. He's outta surgery and we can see him now.'

    I scrolled to Alex's messages and read them. The first three were one long message about how it went at the court. The fourth was asking where Jess and I were. The fifth was asking if Jess was okay. I'm guessing my aunt and uncle called my mom. The last was saying he was at the hospital. I replied, 'Okay. I'll be out soon. I'm in with Jess.'

    I shut my phone and slid it back in my pocket. I turned my attention back to Jess. "He said it went okay. But now he's here waiting to see you." He squeezed my hand. "He's the only one that knows." I didn't want to tell people about Jess. Especially not now. "Sarah's worried about you, too." He nodded.

I felt my phone vibrate and pulled it out. It vibrated again as I flipped it open. Alex said, 'Take your time. You should sit with him for a while.'

I replied, 'I don't want to take up anyone else's time. I'll be out soon.'

I opened Sarah's. Hers said, 'I'm here. I just heard that you were there. Are you okay?'

I replied a simple 'Yeah, I'm alright.' and slid my phone back in my pocket.

"Are you okay?" Jess asked.

"Yeah," I replied. "Just tired. Sarah, my aunt, my uncle, and Alex are here."

"Yeah?" he asked.

I nodded. He smiled and squeezed my hand. I kissed his lips. "I'm sure they all want to see you, Jess." I stood and wrapped my arms around his neck.

He wrapped his around me. "Are you sure?"

I pulled away before he pulled me back. I nodded. "I have to let everyone else get a turn. I'm not going anywhere so I'll see you soon." I smiled down at him.

"Okay. I'll see you soon, Sammi," he added. I kissed his lips again, and moved from him, to the door. "Oh and Sammi, I like the shirt." He smiled.

I returned it, walked out into the hallway, and to the doctor. He guided me back to the waiting room, where I was attacked in hugs.

Sarah and Alex pulled away. "Hey, Sammi. How are you doing?" Alex asked.

I nodded. "I'm okay. He's up if you guys would like to go see him." Sarah nodded and headed towards the doctor, who led her out.

"Are you okay?" Alex asked. I nodded. Until Jess gets better, I guess that was just gonna have to be a question I'd need to get used to.

Chapter 23

I flew up out of my seat. My eyes adjusted and I realized I was in the waiting room. I laid my hands over my face, and tried to calm my breathing and heart rate. I had seen the events of yesterday play for the second time since I fell asleep. I pulled out my phone. It was 6:09 a.m.

I took Jess's hoodie, that Mrs. Isabella gave me, off of my lap and slid it on my arms. Stretching, I walked to the vending machine, and put in a dollar-fifty. I pushed the code for the water, and grabbed it when it dropped. I took a long swig and went to sit back down next to a sleeping Mrs. Isabella.

My aunt took Alex home, Mr. Frank took Sarah home, and my mom and uncle went to work to take care of things in the office.

I took another sip of my water, and tried to process everything that had happened in the past twelve hours. *Jess was attacked by his parents and uncle. Jess wouldn't fight back. He's hurt pretty bad, yet everyone keeps asking if I'm okay.* I shook my head. I wanted to cry all over again. I've never had a scarier nightmare than yesterday's reality.

I pulled out my phone and saw my mom, Alex, Sarah, and Jess had texted me. I went down the line, from newest to oldest. My mom said she loves me and will see me later. I replied, 'Okay. Love you.' Sarah and Alex just said to make sure I relax and get some sleep. I sent back two 'Okay's. Jess said to get some sleep and not to worry about him. He hoped I would sleep well, and to text him when I got up. Then a 'Good night, Sammi.'

I smiled as I read his message. He was really hurt, but he still was checking on me. No one can ever say Jess was not strong. He had to be one of the strongest people I knew. I texted him a 'Good morning.' I didn't know what to do just then. I became anxious, and began rubbing my palms along my thighs. My leg began to shake. I just felt overwhelmed. I prayed that Jess would be healed in miraculous ways, physically and mentally. For our families' peace of mind, and that my friends were okay when they eventually did hear about Jess. I tried to think about all the good The Lord had done. God had been good. It would have been so easy to blame God for what had happened, but no matter what, this wasn't God and his plan, but he would surely make this situation good. Jess's life has been a true tale of injustice, but through faith, I know God will make it good. I know Jess will be rewarded for all of his trials that he passed. Despite these things, I felt I'd be consumed by all of my anxiety. I straightened up to a text. I pulled my phone out and saw it was from Jess. 'Hey, Sammi. Did you just wake up?'

I replied, 'Yeah.'

'How'd you sleep in the chair?' he asked.

I smiled. 'How did you know I'm still at the hospital?'

'Because I know you.'

I smiled again. 'I slept okay.' I didn't mention the nightmare to him because he didn't need to worry about me anymore than he already was.

'Riiiiiiight,' he replied back. I smiled at the playful sarcasm.

'How are you feeling?' I asked.

'I'm alright. They let me go to sleep around 12:30.'

'That's good,' I answered. 'Did you sleep okay?'

'Well, my mattress was a little hard, but it was okay.' I could feel him smile.

Next to me, Mrs. Isabella had woken up. "Hello, sweetheart." She adjusted herself and kissed my temple. "How'd you sleep?" "Okay," I replied.

"Any nightmares?" she asked. I shook my head. Technically, it wasn't a nightmare because it happened. "Did you dream about it?" I sighed and slowly nodded. "I heard your breathing." She smiled down at me.

"Jess is up," I said, desperately wanting to change the subject.

"Yeah?" She asked. I nodded. "You wanna ask if we can see him?" I nodded again. We both stood and moved to the nurse's desk. "May we see, Jesse Jackson?"

"One moment, please." The nurse stood and disappeared behind the double doors. When she came out, she said,

"Follow me." We did and walked back to Jess' room.

Mrs. Isabella ran to Jess and kissed his forehead. "Hi, honey. How are you feeling?" She laid her hand on the side of his face.

"I'm okay." He smiled up at her. If you didn't know Mrs. Isabella was Jess's aunt, you never would have known she wasn't actually his mother. She had a maternal bond with Jess some real mothers don't even have with their child, as was shown. She looked just like him too. Same wavy brunette hair. Same green eyes. Same smile.

"I'll be back," I said, wanting to give them some time alone. I went into the hallway and down the staircase, following the cafeteria signs. When I got there, I went to the counter and purchased a raspberry ice tea, Jess' favorite sports drink, and a coffee with two pumps of creamer and one sugar. I made my way back to the room and entered. Mrs. Isabella and Jess both smiled. I gave Mrs. Isabella her coffee, Jess his drink, and sat in the empty seat by the window with my tea. "Thanks," they both said. I nodded, swinging my legs over one arm.

Mrs. Isabella asked about how the nurses and doctors were treating Jess and things like that. Eventually, her phone went off, and she excused herself to walk in the hallway. I moved to the seat next to his bed. I saw Jess smile, but it was different. There was pain hidden on his face. "Please be honest with me, Jess. How are you feeling?" I slid my hand into his.

He looked into my eyes and stayed silent for a moment. Then, he sighed. He looked away and said, "It hurts a bit"

"And that's okay, Jess." I kissed his cheek and he faced me again. "You're entitled to it. Just because you feel pain, it doesn't make you weak. You're so strong, Jess."

"And so are you." He squeezed my hand. "I honestly don't know who could have done what you did, yesterday." I didn't really know what to say. I did what I had to do to help Jess. That was all. "I know you probably don't believe me, but you should know that you are so much stronger than you believe. I don't know what I'd do without you giving me strength."

I smiled. It was odd. He'd always given me strength. To hear he thought it was the other way around was ... strange. I laid my head down on his right shoulder. He kissed my forehead and wrapped his arm around me, laying his hand on my hip. "I'm glad you're okay, Jess." I felt a tear fall.

"I am, thanks to you. You saved me, Sammi," he replied. I know I should have believed him, but me? Saving him?

I wanted to change the conversation, so I said, "None of our friends know yet, Jess." I felt him nod. "At first, I just didn't want to retell the story, but then I didn't want to tell anyone until I heard how you felt."

He was silent for a while. I heard him let out a deep breath. "I don't want to worry anyone, but I do need the prayers." I nodded. "But you don't have to tell them. I can."

I picked my head up from his shoulder. "I will. You just focus on getting better, Jess." I kissed his cheek and smiled.

"There's that beautiful smile I feel in love with," he said with a light chuckle.

My smile grew and I blushed. Then, Mrs. Isabella walked in and I stood to give her seat back. "No, Sammi. You can stay there."

"That's okay. I have to text some people and let them know how Jess is," I replied. I kissed Jess's forehead once again, and then moved to the seat by the window. I saw Mrs. Isabella sit down next to Jess.

I pulled my phone out and wrote, "Hey, everyone. I'm sorry if you've been trying to reach me and I haven't been answering. I've been so busy. Yesterday, Jess got hurt. He was in serious condition, and now he's in the hospital on Eighth Street. He will be okay and go back to normal, but it'll take time. In the meantime, he needs prayers for healing. Talk to you all soon. If I don't answer you back right away, I will eventually. Thanks, guys." Then, I sent it to everyone who needed to know. I let out a deep breath.

Jess looked over at me momentarily. "Did you do it?" I nodded. "What'd you say?"

I moved next to him and held my phone out for him. He read it. "You did great, Sammi." He smiled up at me.

I saw Mrs. Isabella watching us with a smile as well. "Thanks, Sammi," she said.

"For what, ma'am?" I asked.

"For being you, sweetie." She smiled brighter. "We are all so blessed to have you."

"I know I am," Jess added. He looked at me in a way that made my heart feel whole for the first time since the incident.

I smiled and blushed. "Thank you, Mrs. Isabella, for helping to raise me this way. Jess, thank you for all that you do for me." I saw them smile. I looked down as my phone went crazy with text messages. "People love you, Jess."

Chapter 24

I walked back up to the doors of the hospital. I felt a chill and pulled his jacket up around me. His cologne brought comfort. I slid my backpack off and checked to make sure everything was there. Jess' pillow, bible, a few of his favorite snacks, a small blanket for me, my headphones and my charger. *Check*, I thought. I put it back on my back when the crowd rushed to see me. All of my friends, my youth pastor, and most of the guys on Jess' basketball and football teams were all standing in the waiting room around me. I was bombarded with questions about yesterday and tried to answer them as well as I could.

"He's okay, everyone. Just banged up a bit. But he'll be fine after he heals." I took a shaky breath trying to keep from getting overwhelmed. I felt my brain trying to pull me in deep and I slid my wall up.

"Hey, Sam." Ms Angie, our youth pastor, came over to meet me. She pulled me into a hug. "Can I speak with you for a bit?" she asked.

"Of course, ma'am." My stomach started tightening in a knot. I followed her back outside the hospital, where we sat on a bench. I sighed and leaned my head back to rest on the bench. I closed my eyes and tried to focus on the cool breeze, brushing against my face. The birds chirping in the trees. *Ground yourself, Sam.*

"How are you?" Angie asked after a moment.

I opened my eyes to glance over to her. She was sitting with one leg up on the bench folded under her other, and her right arm on the back of the bench, her hand holding her face steady. I mirrored her and looked into my lap. "I don't really know..."

Ms. Angie nodded slightly. "There's been a lot happening lately. I can't imagine how difficult it's been on you and your friends. Or your mind," She paused and I felt her looking into my face. "How's your PTSD been, Sam? Any flashbacks?"

I sighed again and put my hands in my lap. I played with my fingers. "It's been hard. Some days I can block it out. Other days..." I let out a breath trying to keep focused on now. "Other days I'm just stuck in the nightmares, or the past, or just can't focus. I've been so dazed and drained. I don't want to keep seeing them..." I choked out as tears pricked my eyes. I focused on my fingers trying to count all the lines separating my knuckles.

Ms. Angie nodded and put her hand on mine. She let me breathe for a moment before beginning. "I know that it seems you have the world on your shoulders. I know that in these overwhelming situations, your brain wants to make you feel you deserve all of this. I know it tried to make you feel responsible for all the bad that's happened before. To try to blame you and make you feel that, somehow, you deserve it." I felt tears start to fall and put my face in my hands. I felt Angie move over and slide her arm around me. I leaned onto her shoulder, feeling my chest swell painfully. "But it's not, Sam. This isn't your fault. You don't deserve this. God isn't mad at you and trying to punish you, even though it feels that way."

    I started to cry and laid my hands and face onto my knees. "It feels like I do. I know I don't and I know it's not God punishing me, but it feels like I do deserve it and that He is punishing me for something." I soaked my hands with my tears and sniffled. My body shook. "I want to be angry or to just stop caring. Maybe it'll stop hurting as much. Maybe I could stop thinking about the past. Maybe the nightmares will stop..." I squeaked out. My throat and nose began to burn as I tried to hold my breath to try to slow my heart rate.

    I felt Ms. Angie rub my back as she listened quietly. After a silent minute or two, she took a deep breath. "I know it's hard, Sam. I can't begin to imagine how much harder it is to deal with all this on top of regular, everyday struggles. I know you hate your heart, too. I know you hate that you care so much deeper than others do. That you feel so much deeper. And I wish I could give you exact answers for how God is going to bless you for these struggles or for how He's gonna take this situation of Satan's and turn it into good. But I can't, sweetie. I can't fit God into my box and explain Him step by step. But what I do know is that God is good. That He hears your cries and sees your tears. That He hurts for you."

    My tears began to slow and my head began to pound. The back of my throat became parched and I wiped my eyes. I sat up straight and looked out to the street and across it to the little playground. "I know this isn't His fault. Or did He wish any of this. I'm just so tired of anytime something happens, Satan is able to just throw everything back in my face. To see every bad moment over and over. To say goodbye to my dying dad, to see Jess as a kid before his aunt and uncle got him," I paused briefly trying to push myself to continue. "Issac, the hospital, hearing Alex's story, Ian's funeral, Jess..." A shiver slid up my spine. "To see everything so vividly all the time. To watch it replay like a movie. To never know what's going to start it. I'm tired." I breathed out. My eyes were burning and I just wanted to drift to sleep.

Ms. Angie leaned her head against mine. "God must know you're strong enough to feel so deeply but to still beat this. I know it's hard. I know you want to give up sometimes, but the world needs you, Sam. God knew that. You may never see why, but the mark you're gonna leave behind will bring stirring and change. I'm always here. So is God. Your family too."

I sniffled. "Thanks, Ms. Angie." She tucked her blonde hair behind her ear and her blue eyes focused on me. She waited patiently for me to try to work out my words. I wiped my tears with the sleeve of my jacket and breathed out heavily. "I want to be healed. I do. I don't wanna be known as the insecure girl who struggles with self image and mental health. The girl who was used and is hated because of her body. The girl without the dad. The girl who fights for ethnic identity and the urge to just give up. The psych ward girl. I don't want that to be my identity."

"Can I pray for ya, Sam?" Angie asked. I nodded and sniffled, closing my eyes. I felt her hand on my shoulder as she began. "God we come before you today, asking for healing. A complete and total healing for Sam. A healing so supernatural that even Satan will sit in absolute awe of Your power. God, we know Satan is attacking Sam because he's afraid of her and what You can do through her. Help Sam remember who she is when those memories come storming back. Help her find the strength she craves. The strength to punch the devil back harder than he hit first."

I felt fresh tears prick my eyes as I listened closely, desperately wanting the words to come true. "There's so much of Your power in her. Block out the lies Satan spews into her ears, the lies she's starting to believe. Give her the self love and confidence that Satan has broken down her whole life. Don't just give her the strength but also the mind to love herself and believe she is strong enough, through You, to leave the past in the past and not give Satan the chance to poke her insecurities because she won't believe she has them. Give her the strength in her mind to know she was created by a God that makes no mistakes. To know she isn't a mistake. God we ask for all this in your name, already thanking you for the healing that's coming. Amen."

    I sniffled. I looked up to the sky and saw clouds forming overhead. Off to the left, there was a break in the clouds in the shape of a lion. Above the lion was a rainbow. I smiled and let out a deep breath. *Thanks, God.*

Hey reader!

I hope through reading this, you feel more valid in your struggles. I hope you feel loved and understood in a way you never have. I hope you feel less alone. I hope you know you matter. I hope you know you are needed. I hope you know it's okay to not have everything figured out. I hope you know you are a beautiful creation. I hope you know you're not a mistake. I hope you know God loves you. I hope you know He sees you and His heart breaks for you in your struggles. I hope you know your past doesn't define you. I hope you know God didn't wish that harm on you. I hope you know that this world needs you.

Remember, you're you and you're beautiful for it!
~Danika~

Made in the USA
Monee, IL
20 July 2021